BABYMOUSE AND FRIENDS*

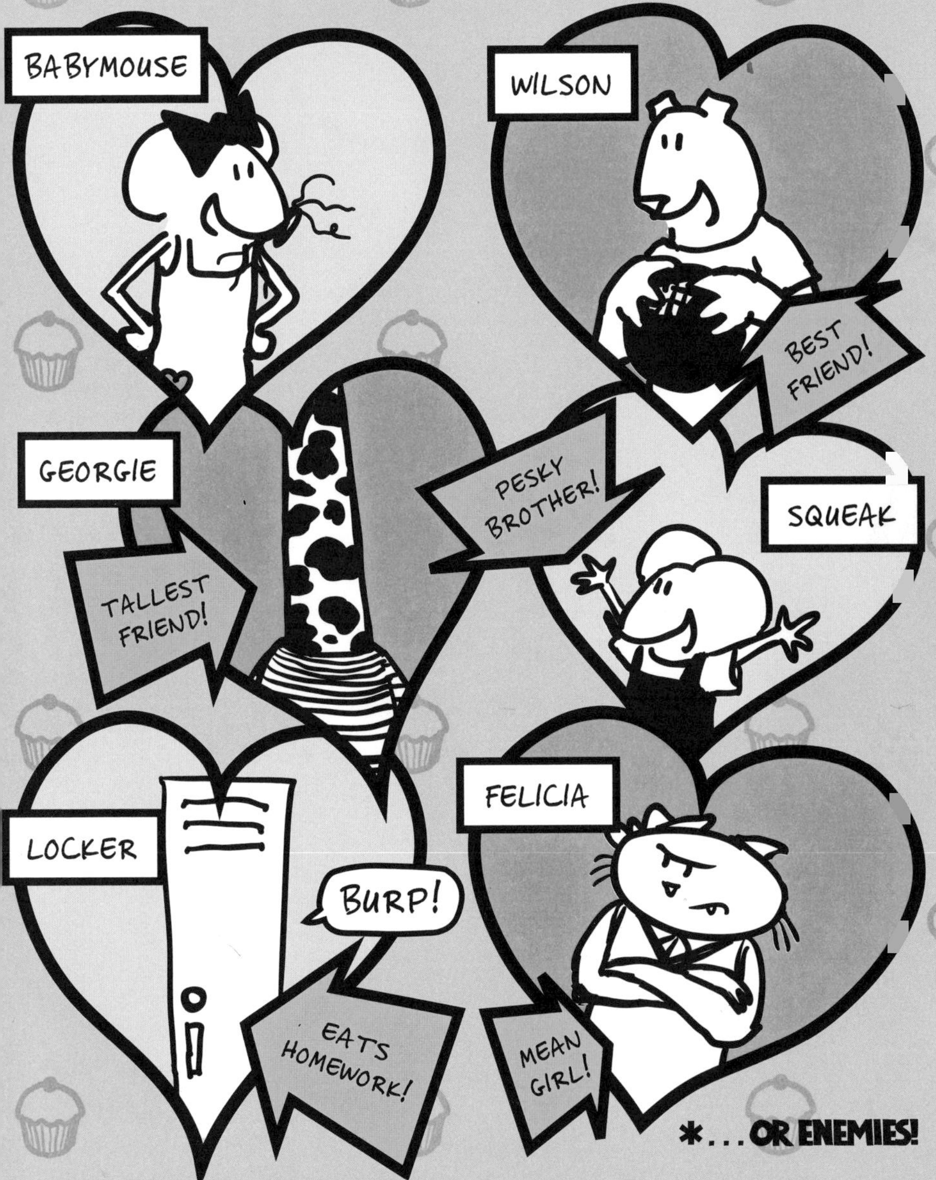
BABYMOUSE
WILSON
BEST FRIEND!
GEORGIE
TALLEST FRIEND!
PESKY BROTHER!
SQUEAK
LOCKER
BURP!
EATS HOMEWORK!
FELICIA
MEAN GIRL!

*. . . OR ENEMIES!

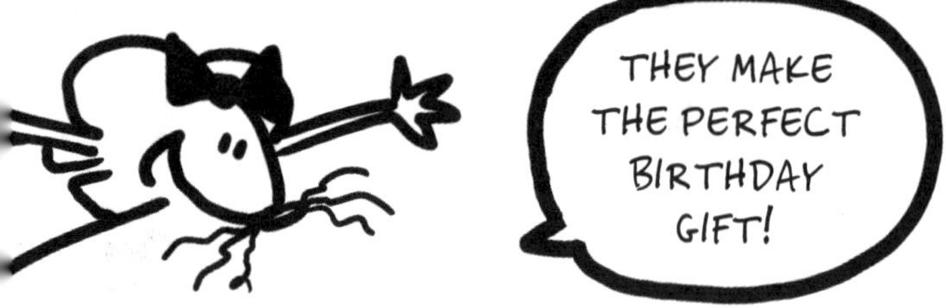
THEY MAKE THE PERFECT BIRTHDAY GIFT!

BE SURE TO READ **ALL** THE **BABYMOUSE** BOOKS:

#1 BABYMOUSE: Queen of the World!
#2 BABYMOUSE: Our Hero
#3 BABYMOUSE: Beach Babe
#4 BABYMOUSE: Rock Star
#5 BABYMOUSE: Heartbreaker
#6 CAMP BABYMOUSE
#7 BABYMOUSE: Skater Girl
#8 BABYMOUSE: Puppy Love
#9 BABYMOUSE: Monster Mash
#10 BABYMOUSE: The Musical
#11 BABYMOUSE: Dragonslayer
#12 BABYMOUSE: Burns Rubber
#13 BABYMOUSE: Cupcake Tycoon
#14 BABYMOUSE: Mad Scientist
#15 A Very BABYMOUSE Christmas
#16 BABYMOUSE for President
#17 Extreme BABYMOUSE
#18 Happy Birthday, BABYMOUSE

HAPPY BIRTHDAY, BABYMOUSE

BY JENNIFER L. HOLM & MATTHEW HOLM

RANDOM HOUSE  NEW YORK

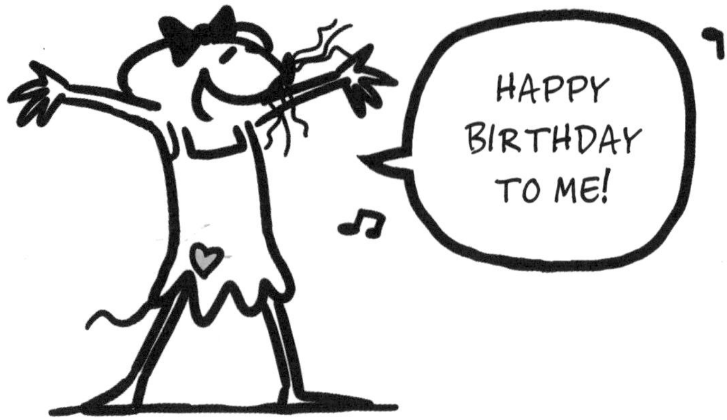
HAPPY BIRTHDAY TO ME!

This is a work of fiction. Names, characters, places, and incidents either are the product of the authors' imagination or are used fictitiously. Any resemblance to actual persons, living or dead, events, or locales is entirely coincidental.

Visit us on the Web!
randomhouse.com/kids
Babymouse.com

Educators and librarians, for a variety of teaching tools, visit us at
RHTeachersLibrarians.com

Library of Congress Cataloging-in-Publication Data
Holm, Jennifer L.
Happy birthday, Babymouse / by Jennifer L. Holm & Matthew Holm. — 1st ed.
p. cm. — (Babymouse ; #18)
Summary: Babymouse imagines the biggest, most wonderful birthday party ever for herself and tries to make it happen, but Felicia is planning her own birthday bash for the very same day.
ISBN 978-0-307-93161-0 (trade pbk.) — ISBN 978-0-375-97097-9 (lib. bdg.) — ISBN 978-0-307-97544-7 (ebook)
1. Graphic novels. [1. Graphic novels. 2. Imagination—Fiction. 3. Birthdays—Fiction. 4. Parties—Fiction. 5. Mice—Fiction.] I. Holm, Matthew. II. Title.
PZ7.7.H65Hap 2013 741.5'973—dc23 2012039798

MANUFACTURED IN MALAYSIA 10 9 8 7 6 5 4 3 2 1 First Edition

Random House Children's Books supports the First Amendment and celebrates the right to read.

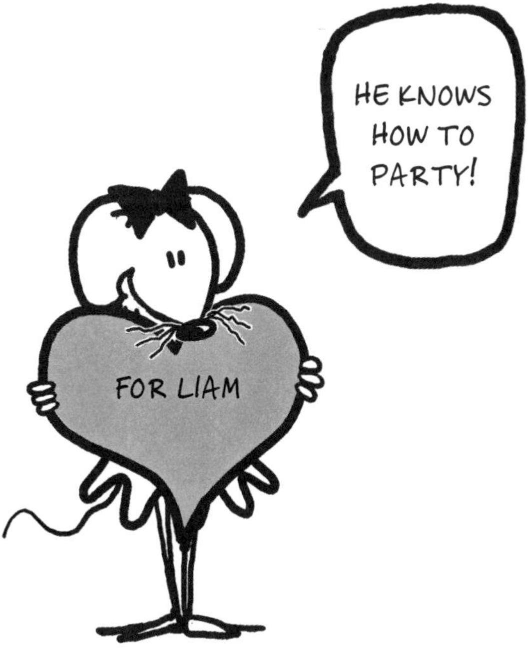
HE KNOWS HOW TO PARTY!
FOR LIAM

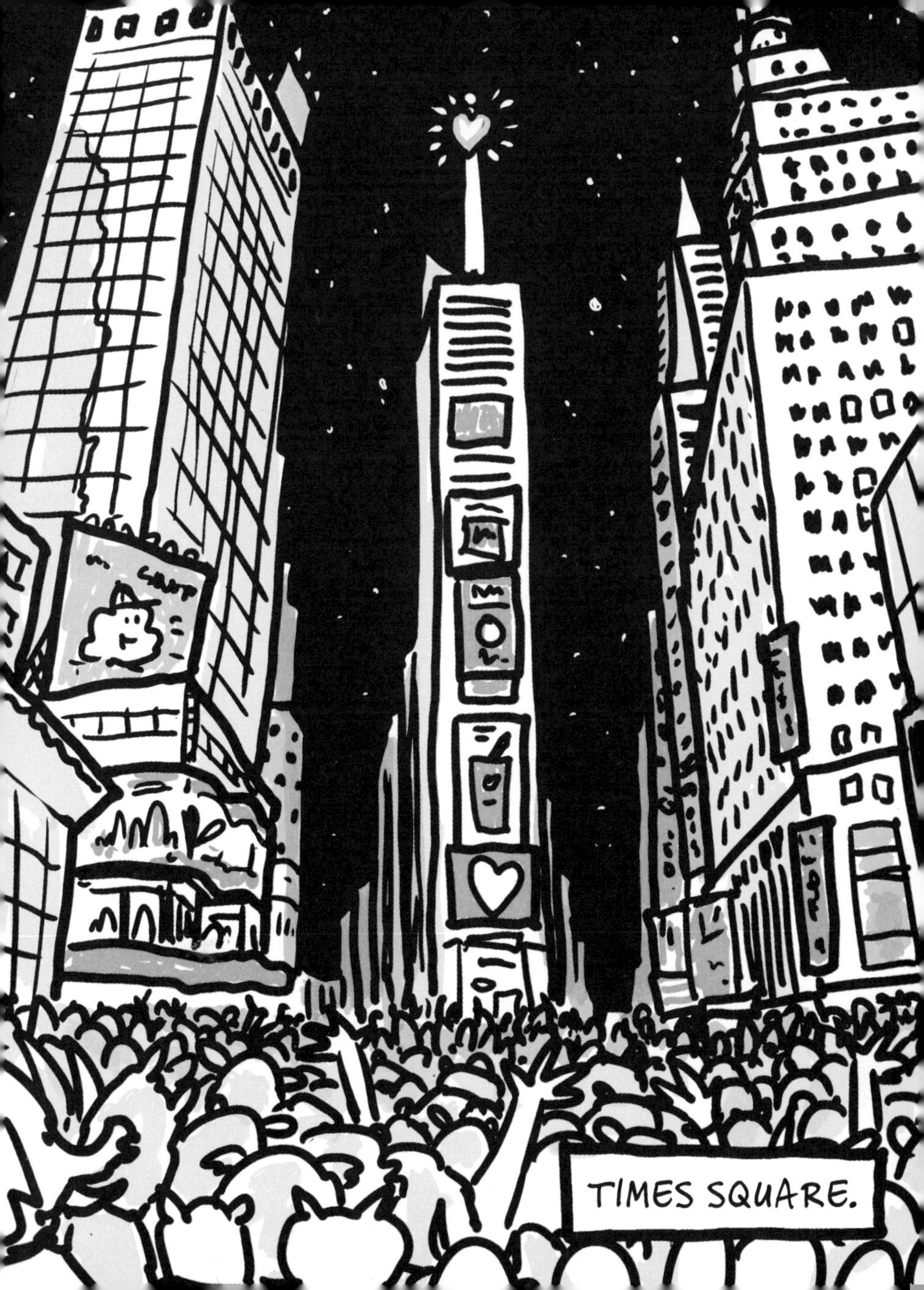
TIMES SQUARE.

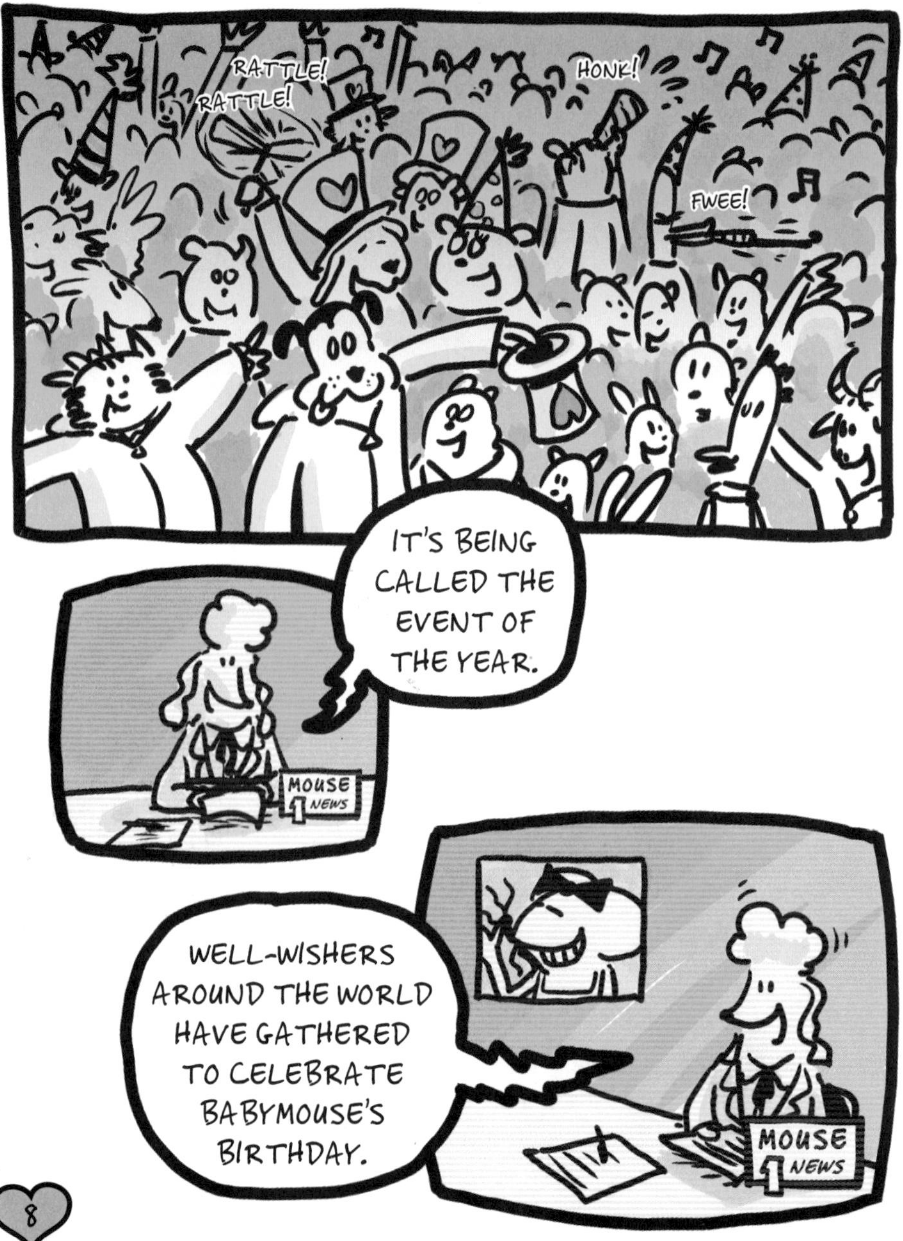
RATTLE!
RATTLE!
HONK!
FWEE!
IT'S BEING CALLED THE EVENT OF THE YEAR.
MOUSE 1 NEWS
WELL-WISHERS AROUND THE WORLD HAVE GATHERED TO CELEBRATE BABYMOUSE'S BIRTHDAY.
MOUSE 1 NEWS

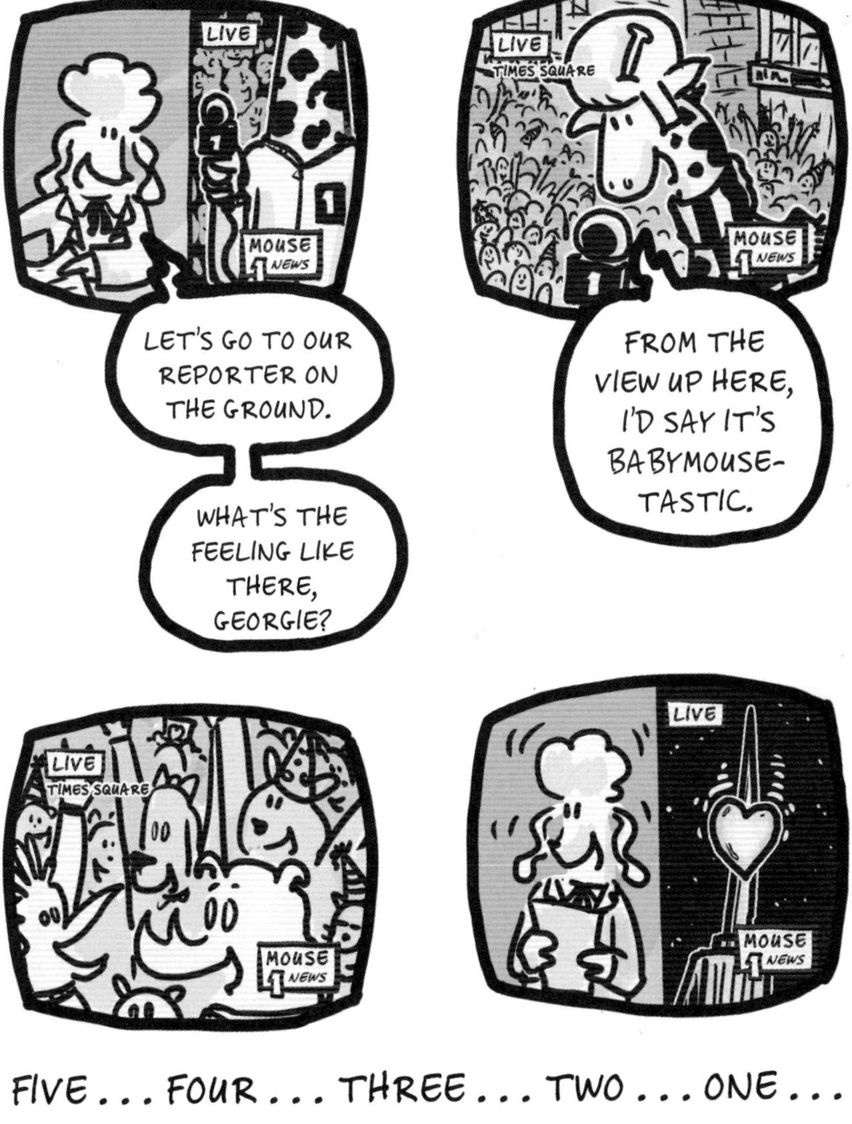
LIVE
MOUSE 1 NEWS
LET'S GO TO OUR REPORTER ON THE GROUND.
WHAT'S THE FEELING LIKE THERE, GEORGIE?
LIVE
TIMES SQUARE
MOUSE 1 NEWS
FROM THE VIEW UP HERE, I'D SAY IT'S BABYMOUSE-TASTIC.
LIVE
TIMES SQUARE
MOUSE 1 NEWS
LIVE
MOUSE 1 NEWS
FIVE . . . FOUR . . . THREE . . . TWO . . . ONE . . .

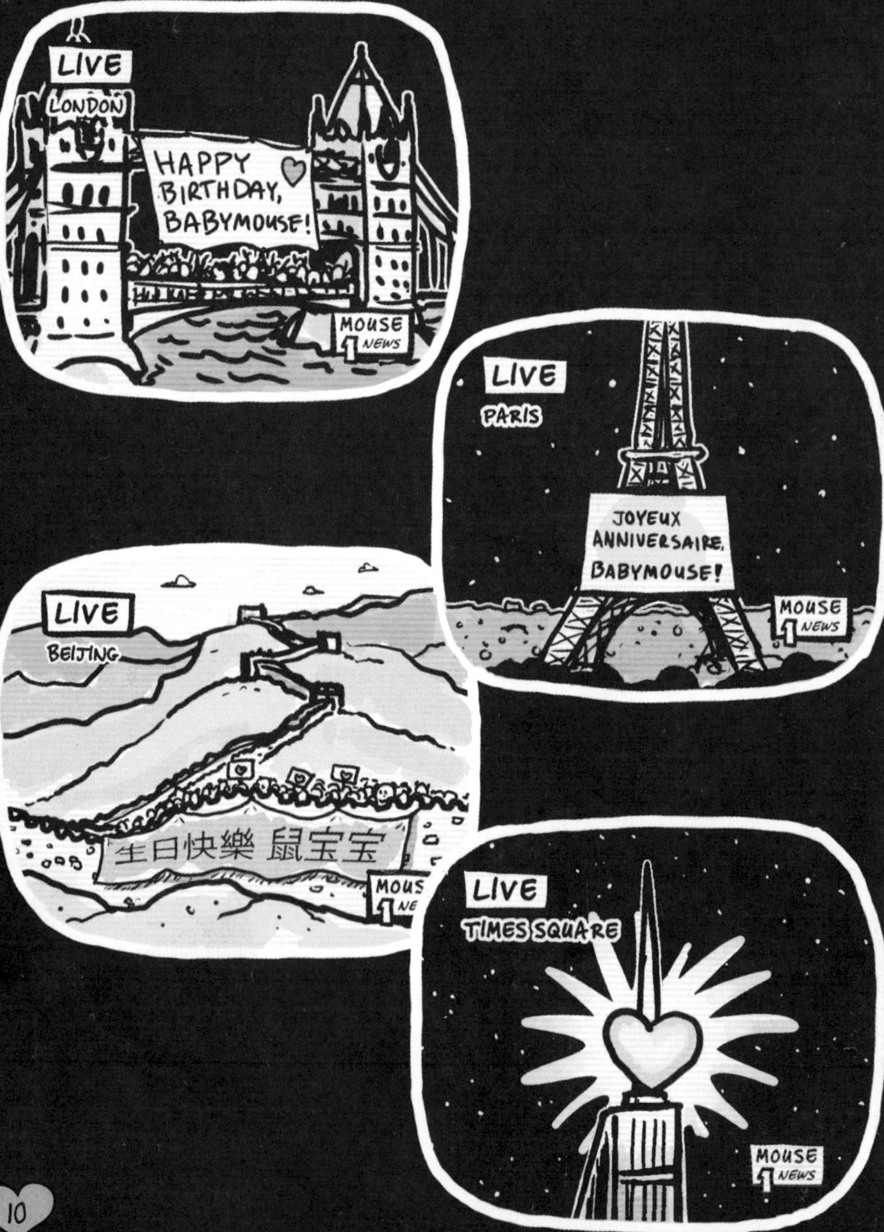
LIVE
LONDON
HAPPY BIRTHDAY, BABYMOUSE!
MOUSE 1 NEWS
LIVE
PARIS
JOYEUX ANNIVERSAIRE, BABYMOUSE!
MOUSE 1 NEWS
LIVE
BEIJING
生日快樂 鼠宝宝
MOUS 1 NE
LIVE
TIMES SQUARE
MOUSE 1 NEWS

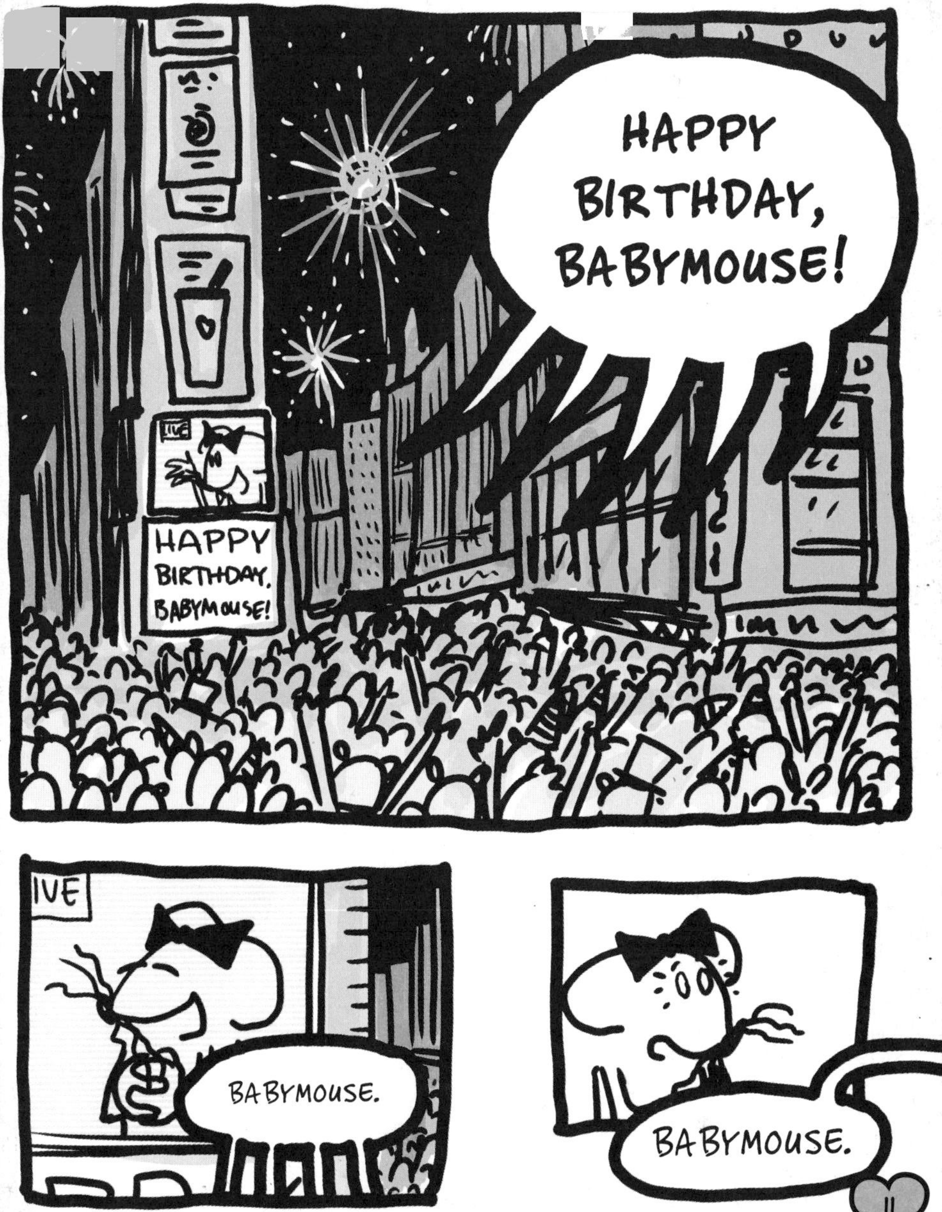
HAPPY BIRTHDAY, BABYMOUSE!
IVE
HAPPY BIRTHDAY, BABYMOUSE!
IVE
BABYMOUSE.
BABYMOUSE.

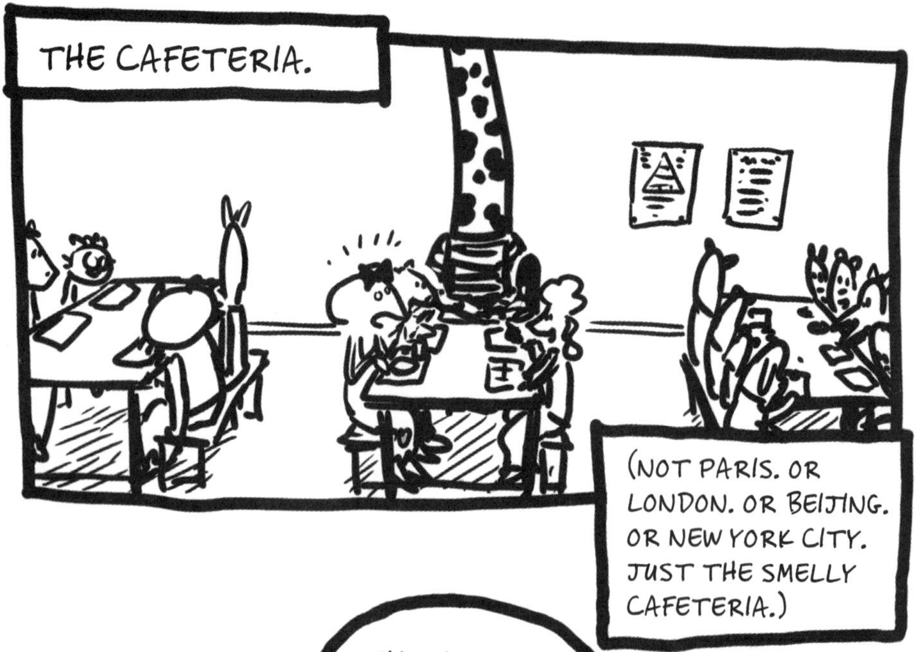
THE CAFETERIA.
(NOT PARIS. OR LONDON. OR BEIJING. OR NEW YORK CITY. JUST THE SMELLY CAFETERIA.)

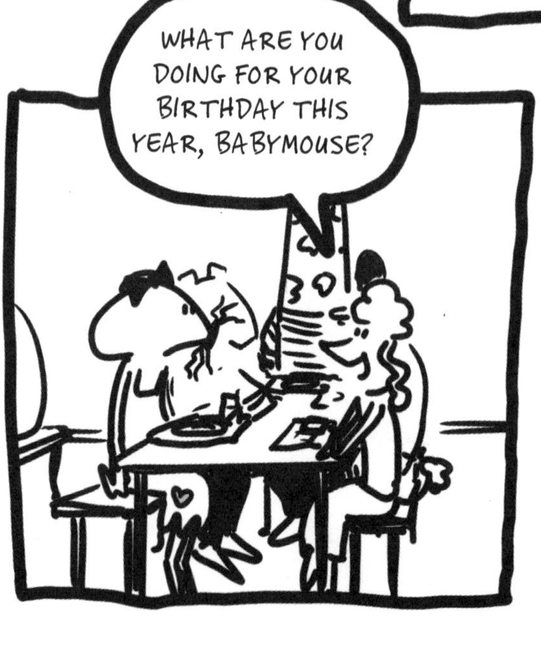
WHAT ARE YOU DOING FOR YOUR BIRTHDAY THIS YEAR, BABYMOUSE?

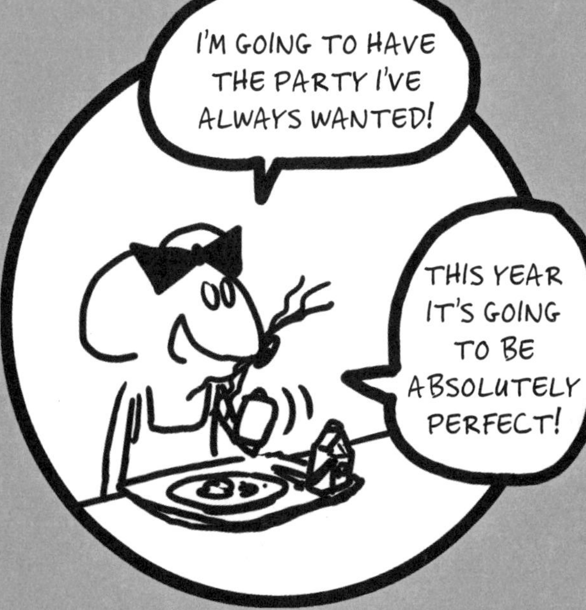
I'M GOING TO HAVE THE PARTY I'VE ALWAYS WANTED!
THIS YEAR IT'S GOING TO BE ABSOLUTELY PERFECT!

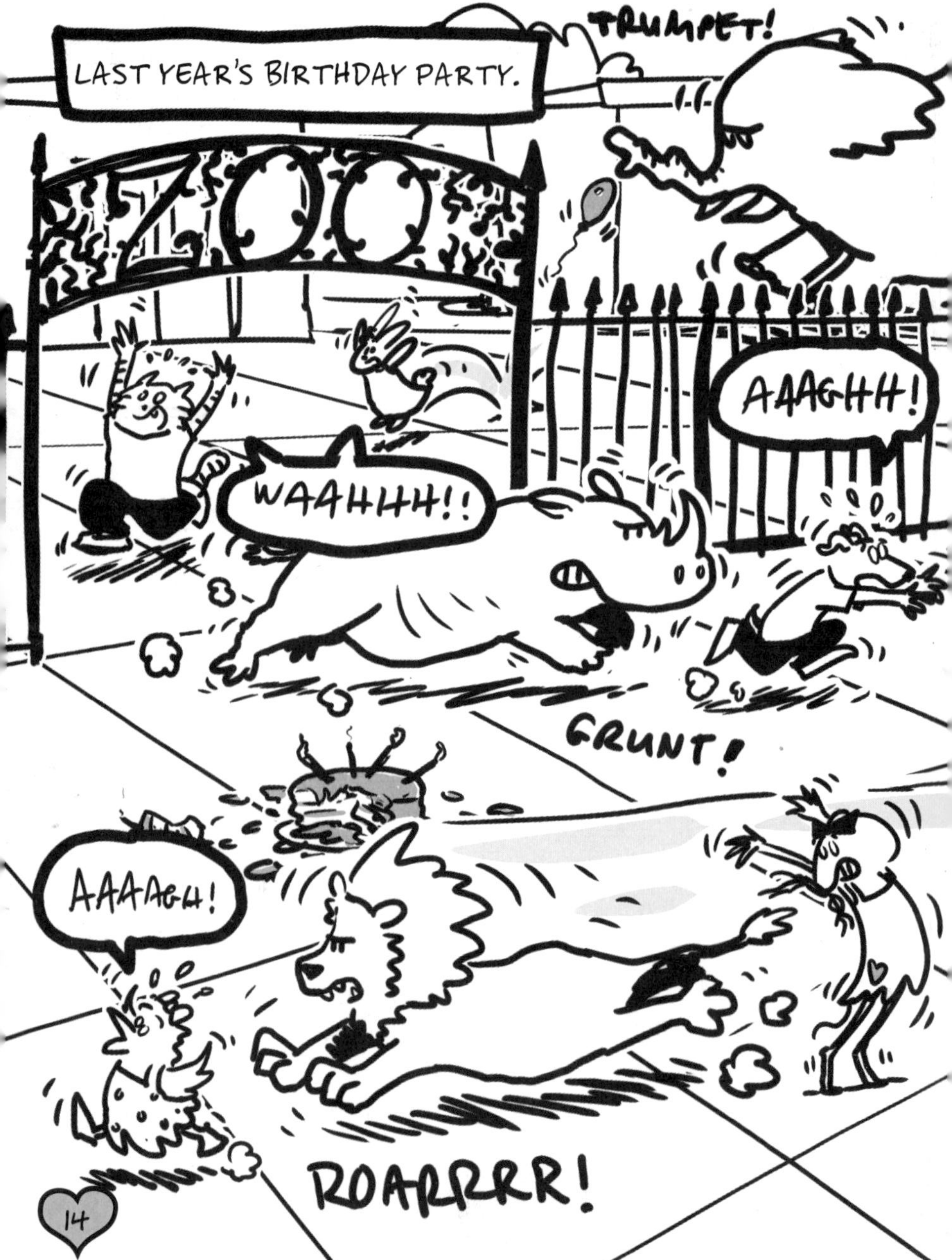
LAST YEAR'S BIRTHDAY PARTY.
ZOO
TRUMPET!
AAAGHH!
WAAHHH!!
GRUNT!
AAAAGH!
ROARRRR!

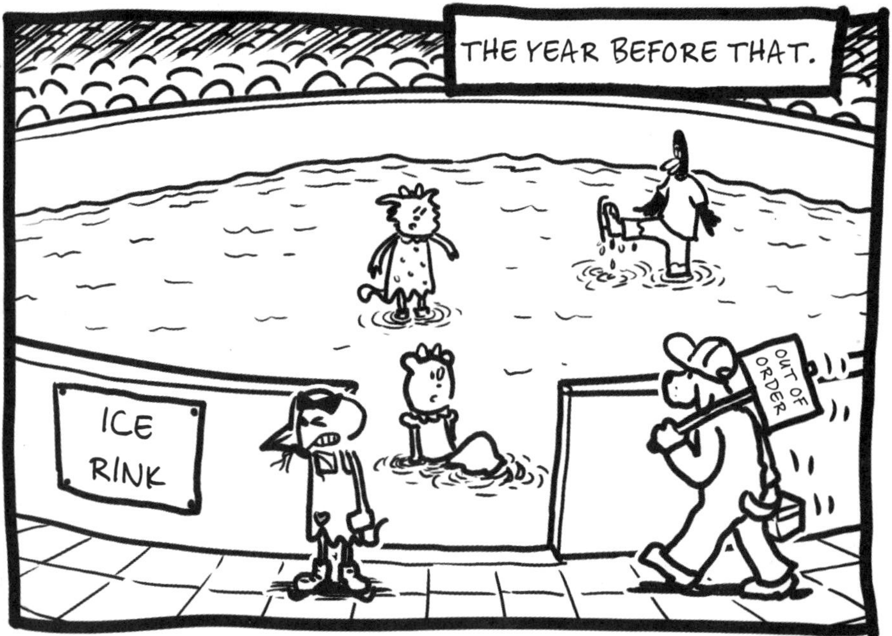
THE YEAR BEFORE THAT.
ICE RINK
OUT OF ORDER

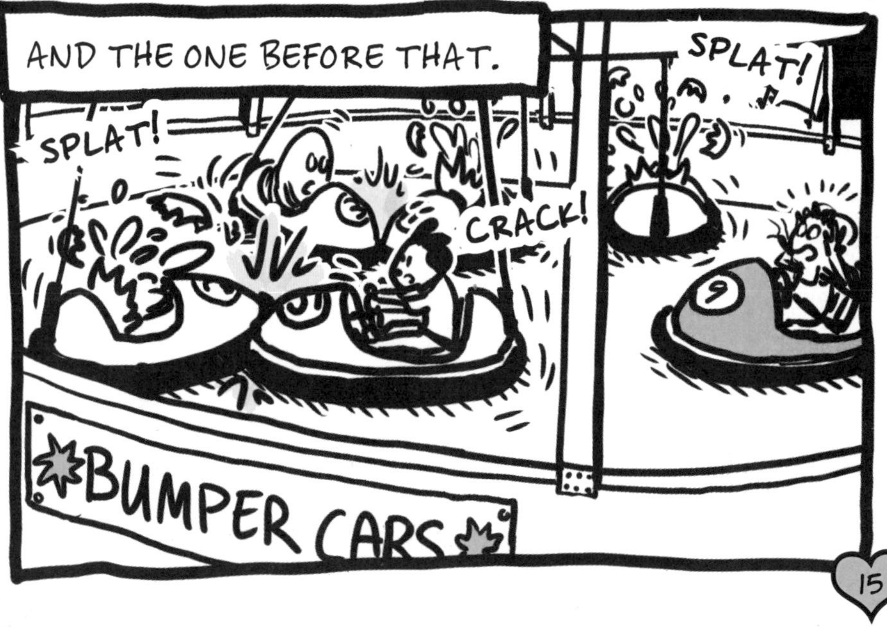
AND THE ONE BEFORE THAT.
SPLAT!
SPLAT!
CRACK!
9
BUMPER CARS

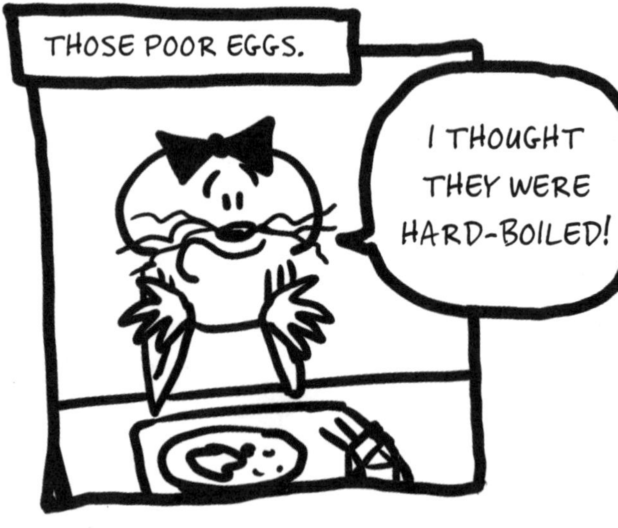
THOSE POOR EGGS.
I THOUGHT THEY WERE HARD-BOILED!

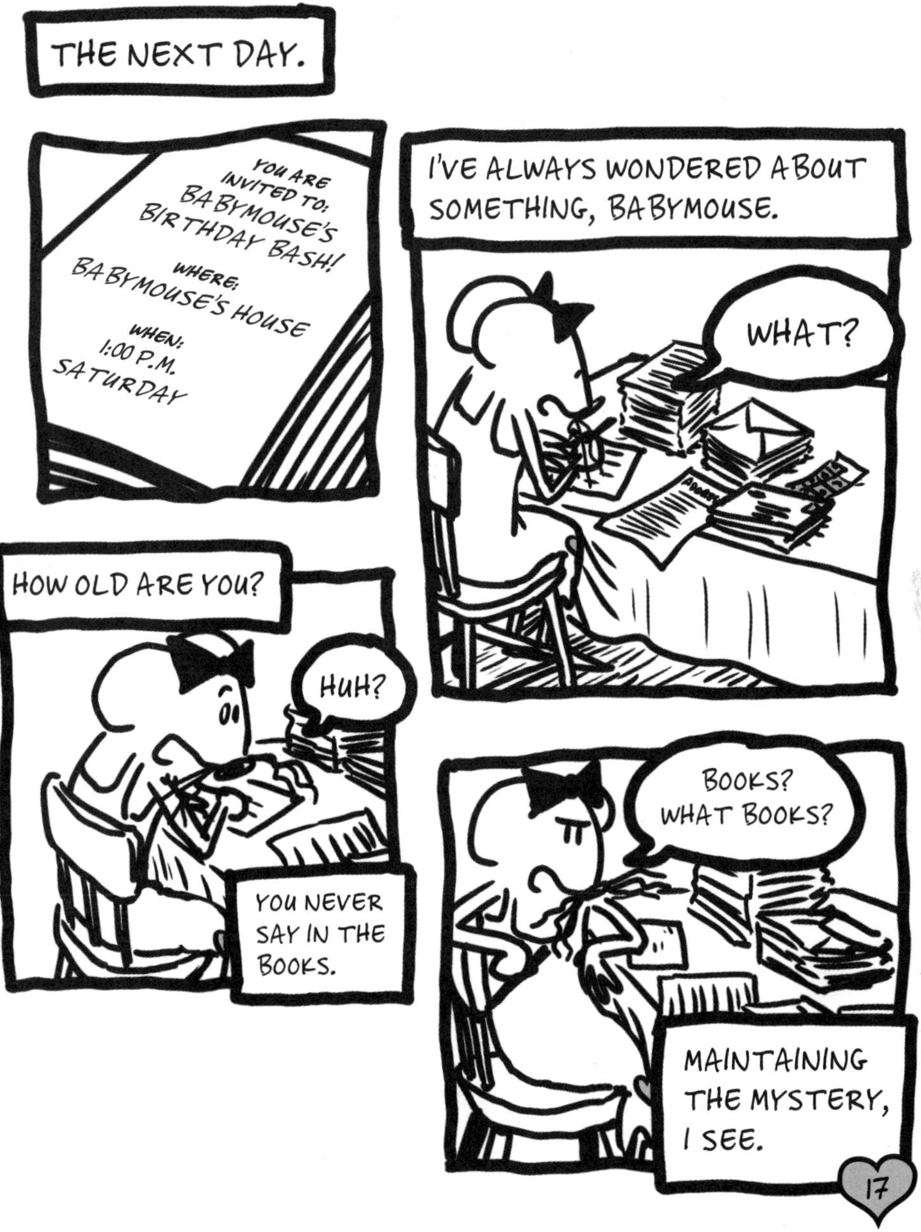
THE NEXT DAY.
YOU ARE INVITED TO: BABYMOUSE'S BIRTHDAY BASH!
WHERE: BABYMOUSE'S HOUSE
WHEN: 1:00 P.M. SATURDAY
I'VE ALWAYS WONDERED ABOUT SOMETHING, BABYMOUSE.
WHAT?
HOW OLD ARE YOU?
HUH?
YOU NEVER SAY IN THE BOOKS.
BOOKS? WHAT BOOKS?
MAINTAINING THE MYSTERY, I SEE.

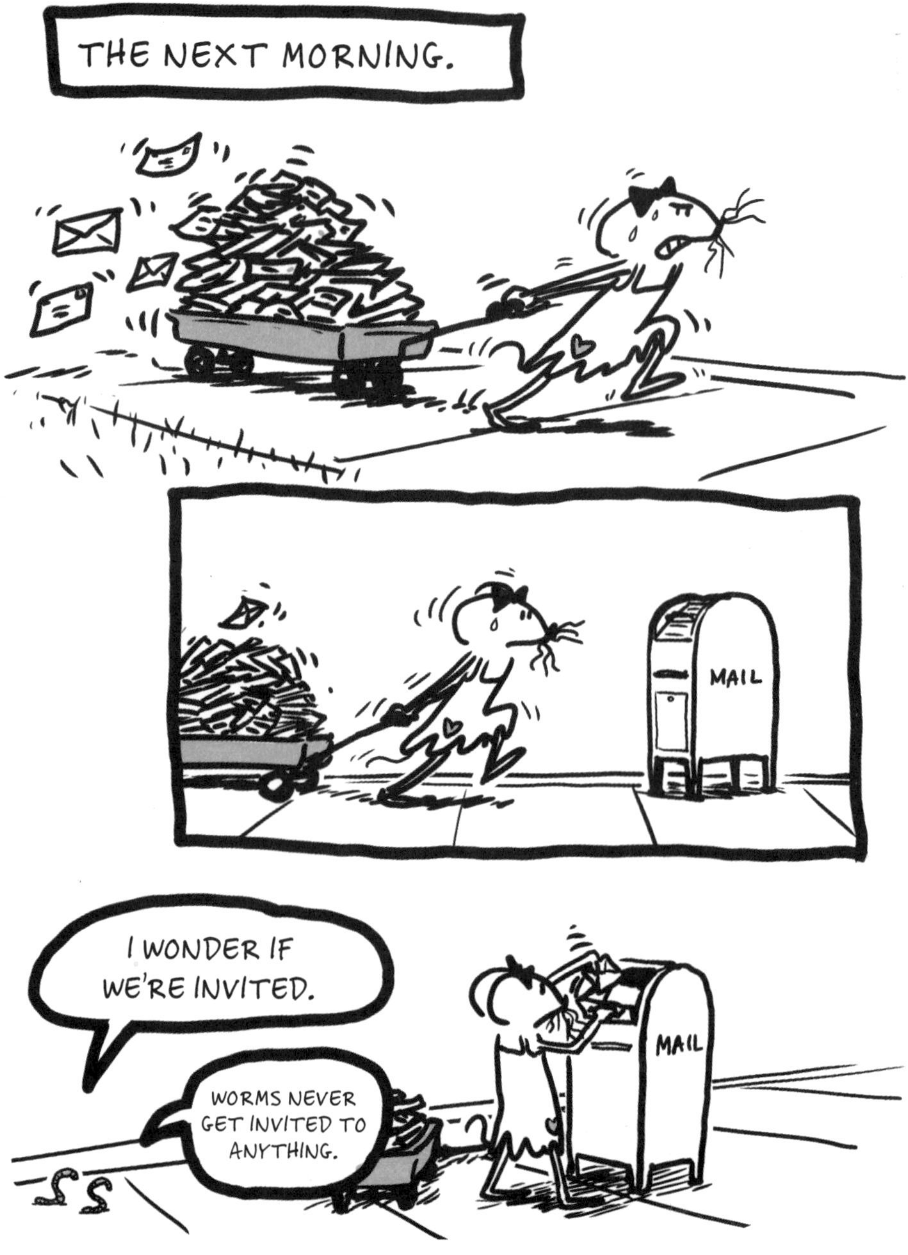
THE NEXT MORNING.
MAIL
MAIL
I WONDER IF WE'RE INVITED.
WORMS NEVER GET INVITED TO ANYTHING.

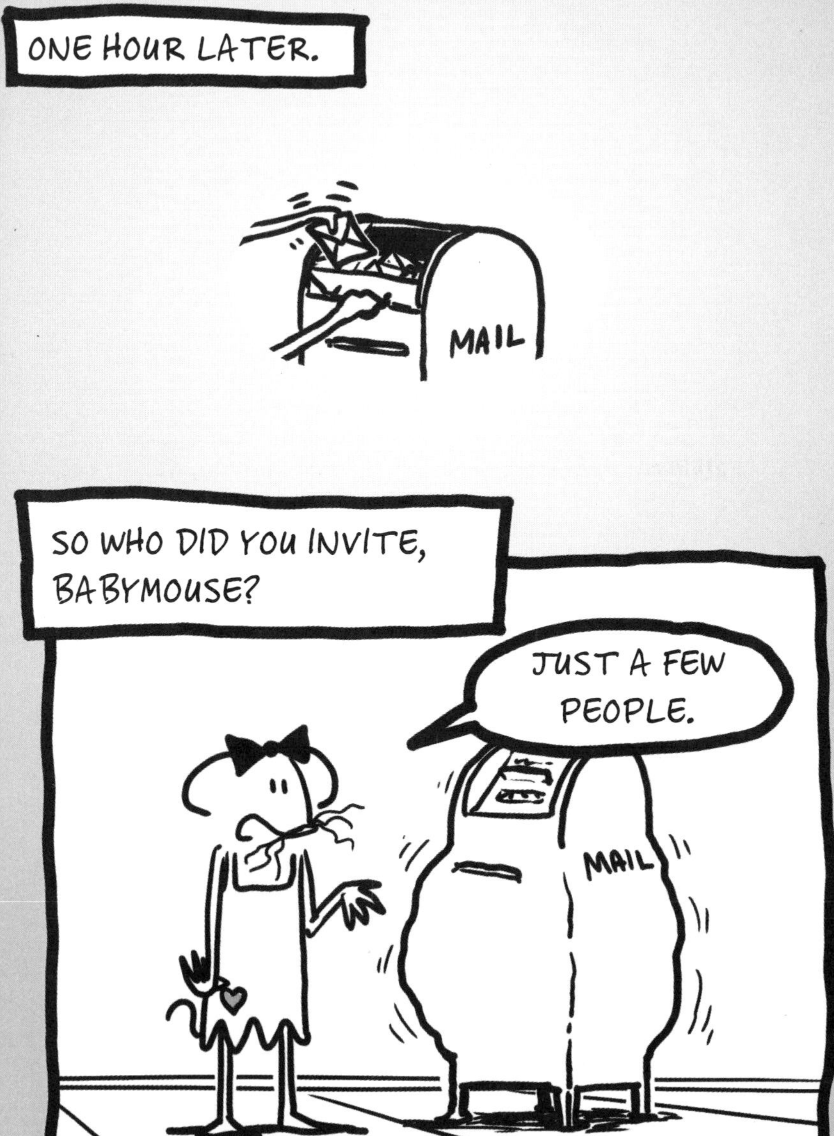
ONE HOUR LATER.
MAIL
SO WHO DID YOU INVITE, BABYMOUSE?
JUST A FEW PEOPLE.
MAIL

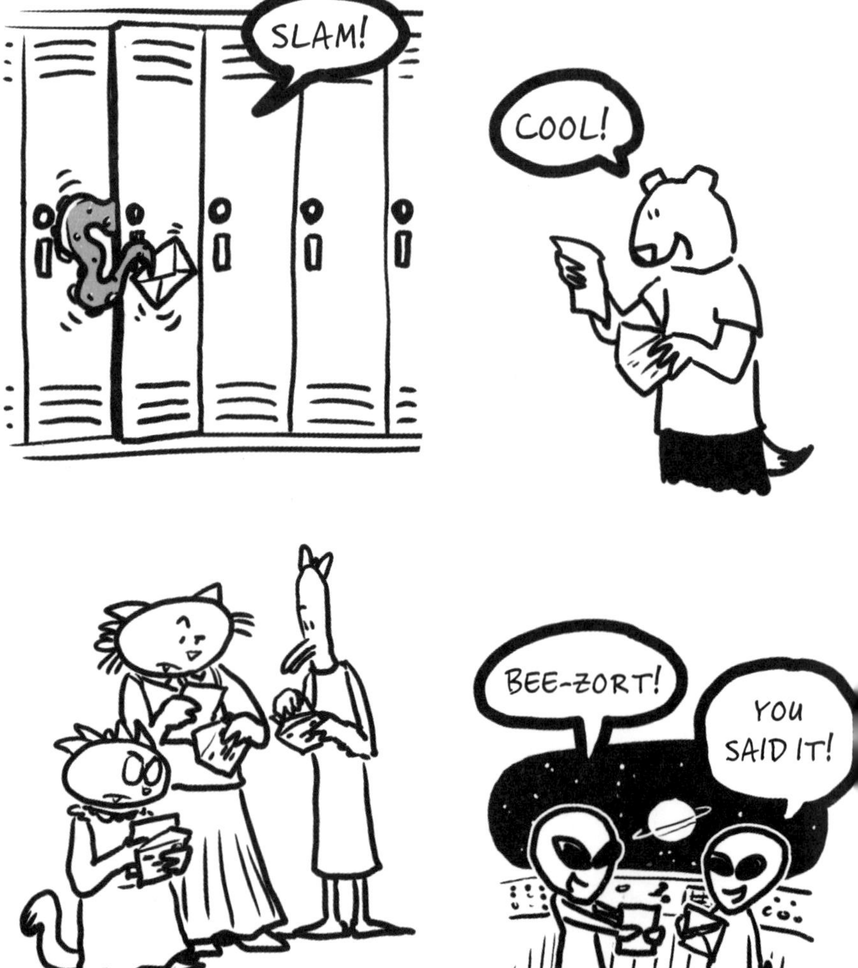
SLAM!
COOL!
BEE-ZORT!
YOU SAID IT!

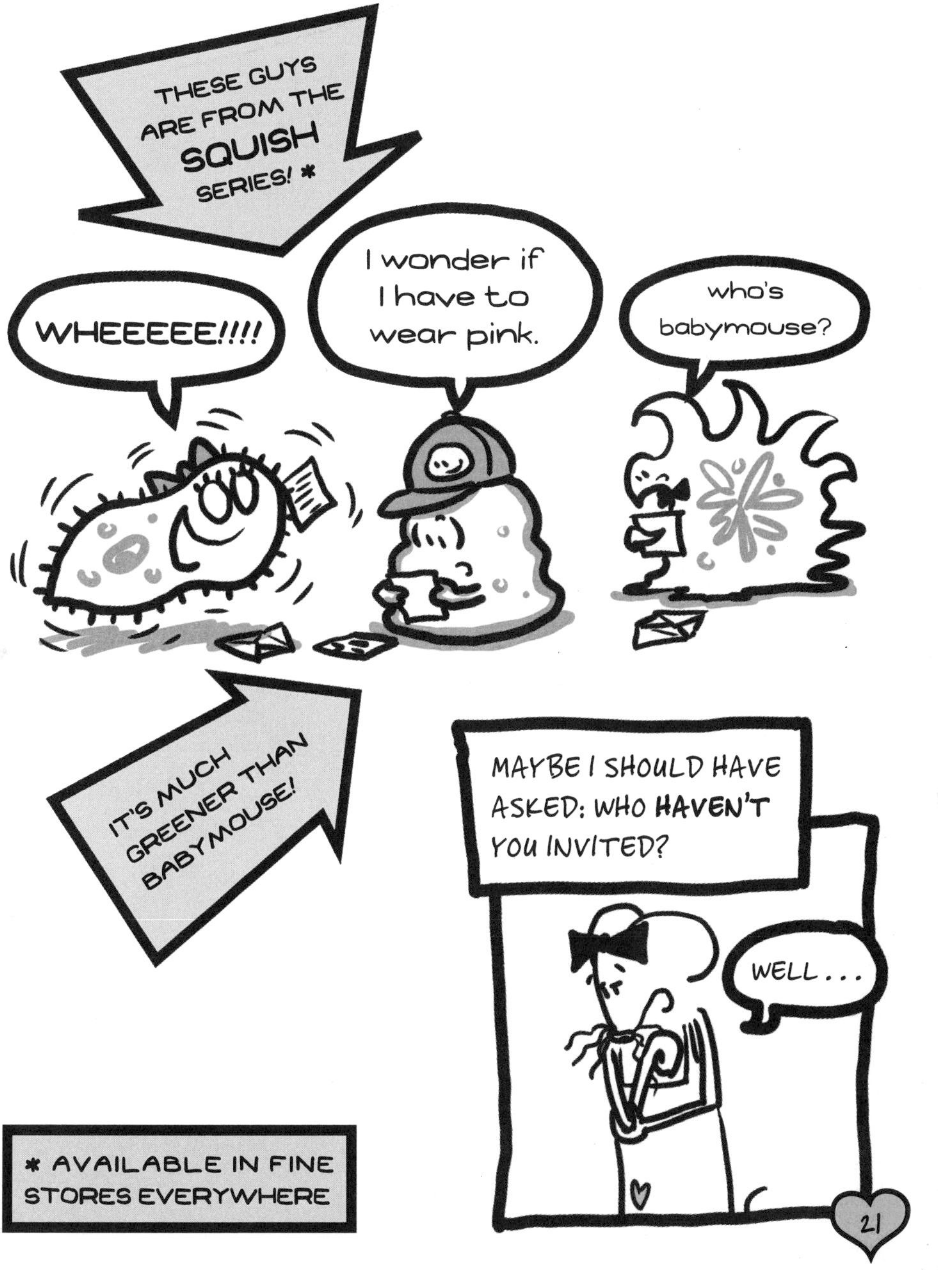

THESE GUYS ARE FROM THE SQUISH SERIES! *
WHEEEEEE!!!!
I wonder if I have to wear pink.
who's babymouse?
IT'S MUCH GREENER THAN BABYMOUSE!
MAYBE I SHOULD HAVE ASKED: WHO HAVEN'T YOU INVITED?
WELL . . .
* AVAILABLE IN FINE STORES EVERYWHERE
21

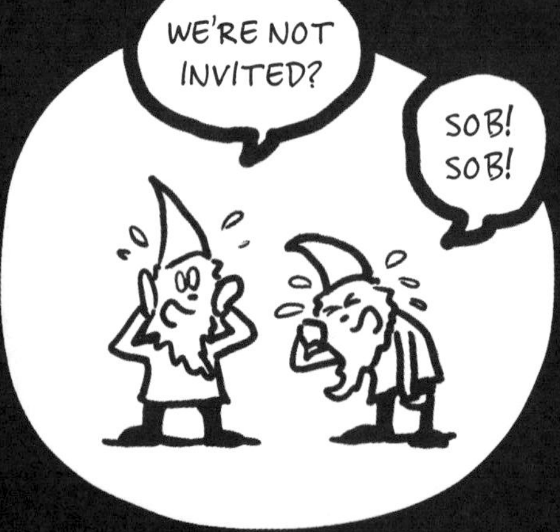
WE'RE NOT INVITED?
SOB! SOB!

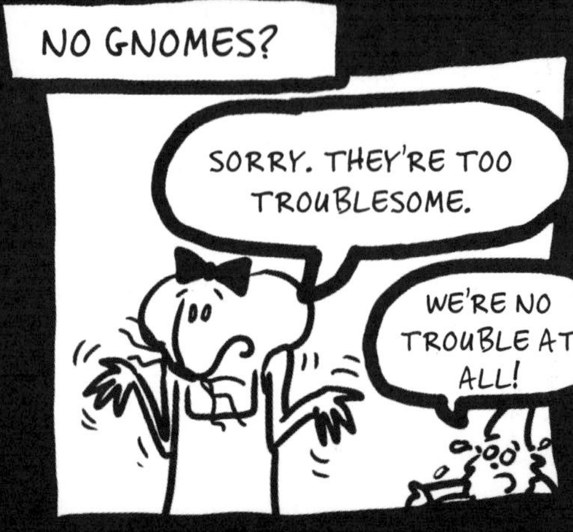
NO GNOMES?
SORRY. THEY'RE TOO TROUBLESOME.
WE'RE NO TROUBLE AT ALL!

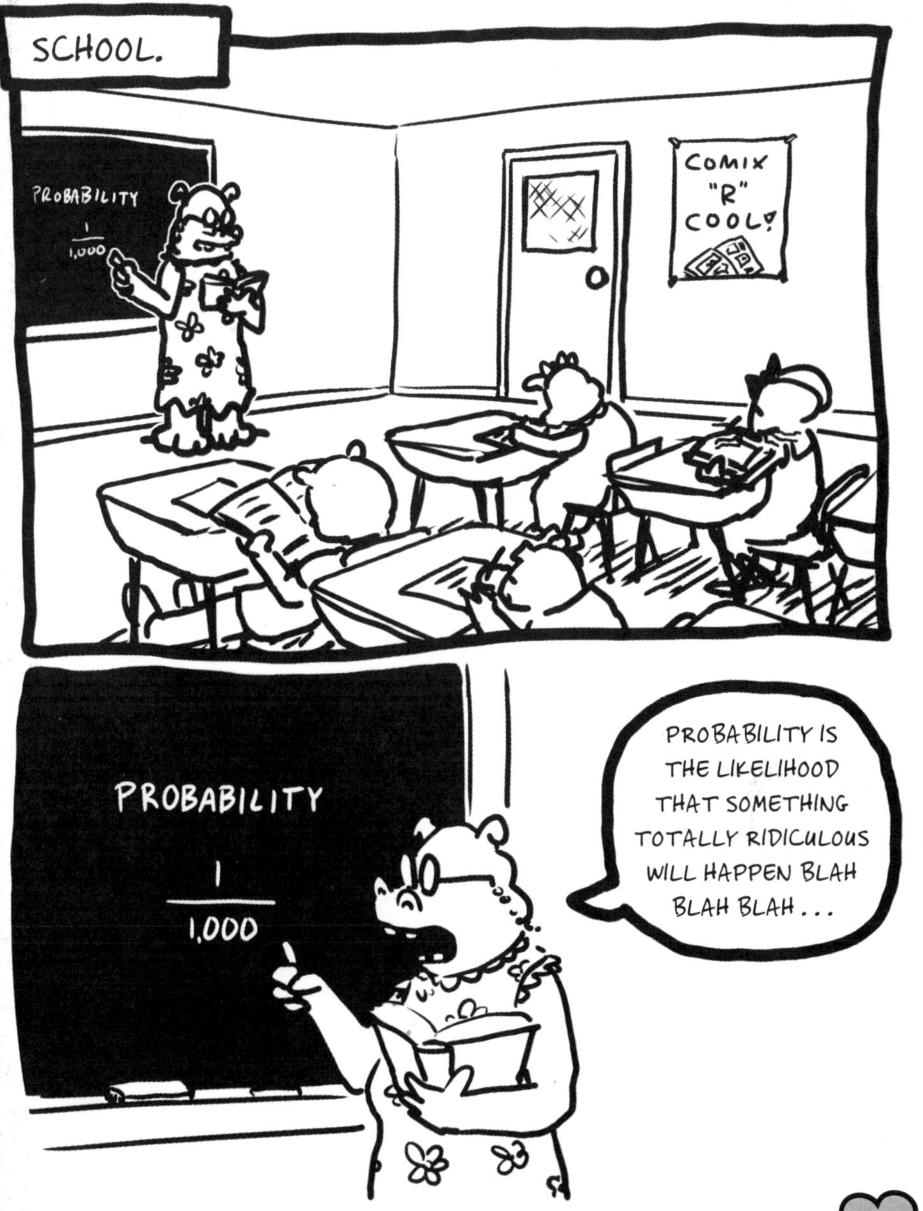
SCHOOL.
PROBABILITY
1
1,000
COMIX "R" COOL!
PROBABILITY
1
1,000
PROBABILITY IS THE LIKELIHOOD THAT SOMETHING TOTALLY RIDICULOUS WILL HAPPEN BLAH BLAH BLAH . . .

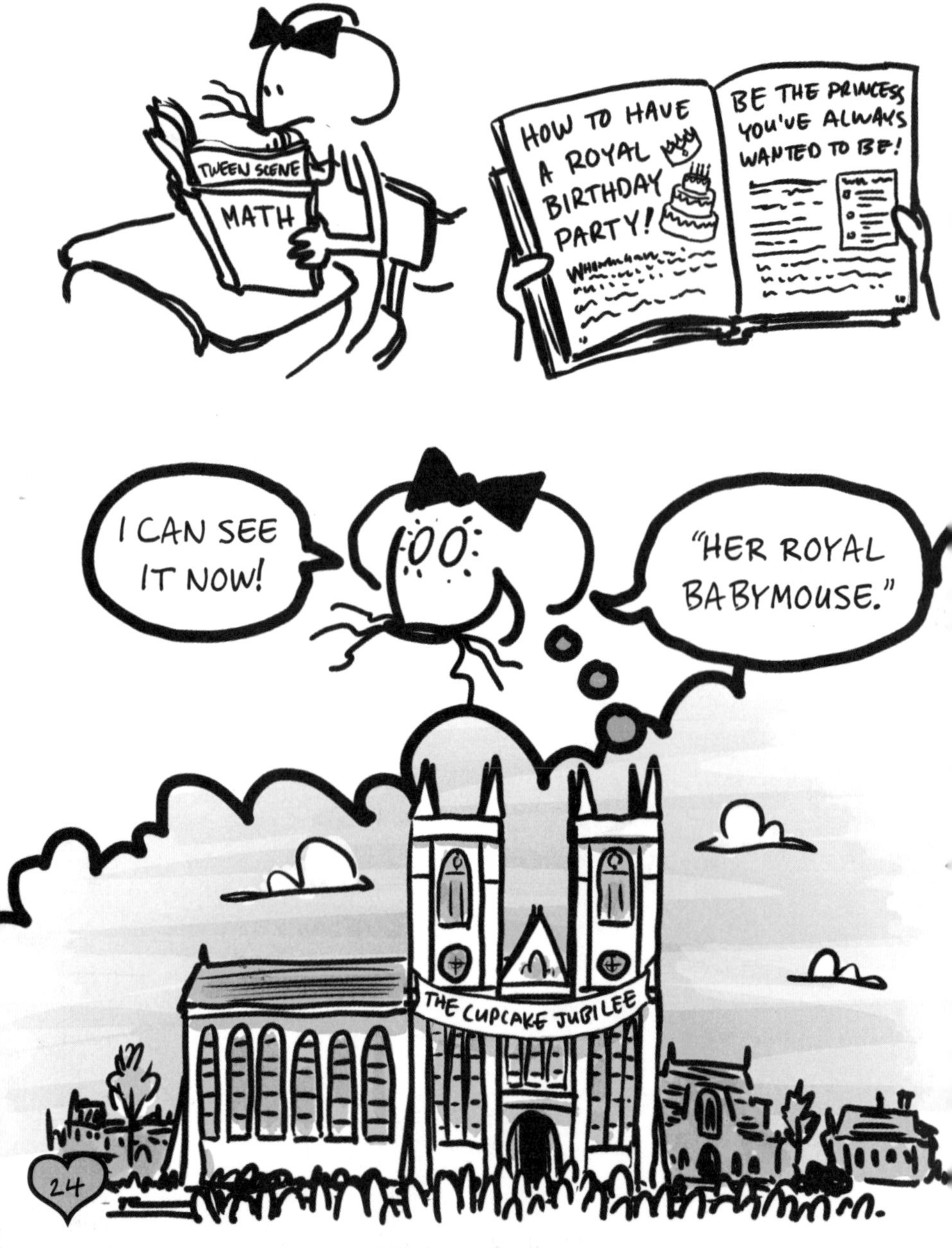
TWEEN SCENE
MATH
HOW TO HAVE A ROYAL BIRTHDAY PARTY!
BE THE PRINCESS YOU'VE ALWAYS WANTED TO BE!
I CAN SEE IT NOW!
"HER ROYAL BABYMOUSE."
THE CUPCAKE JUBILEE

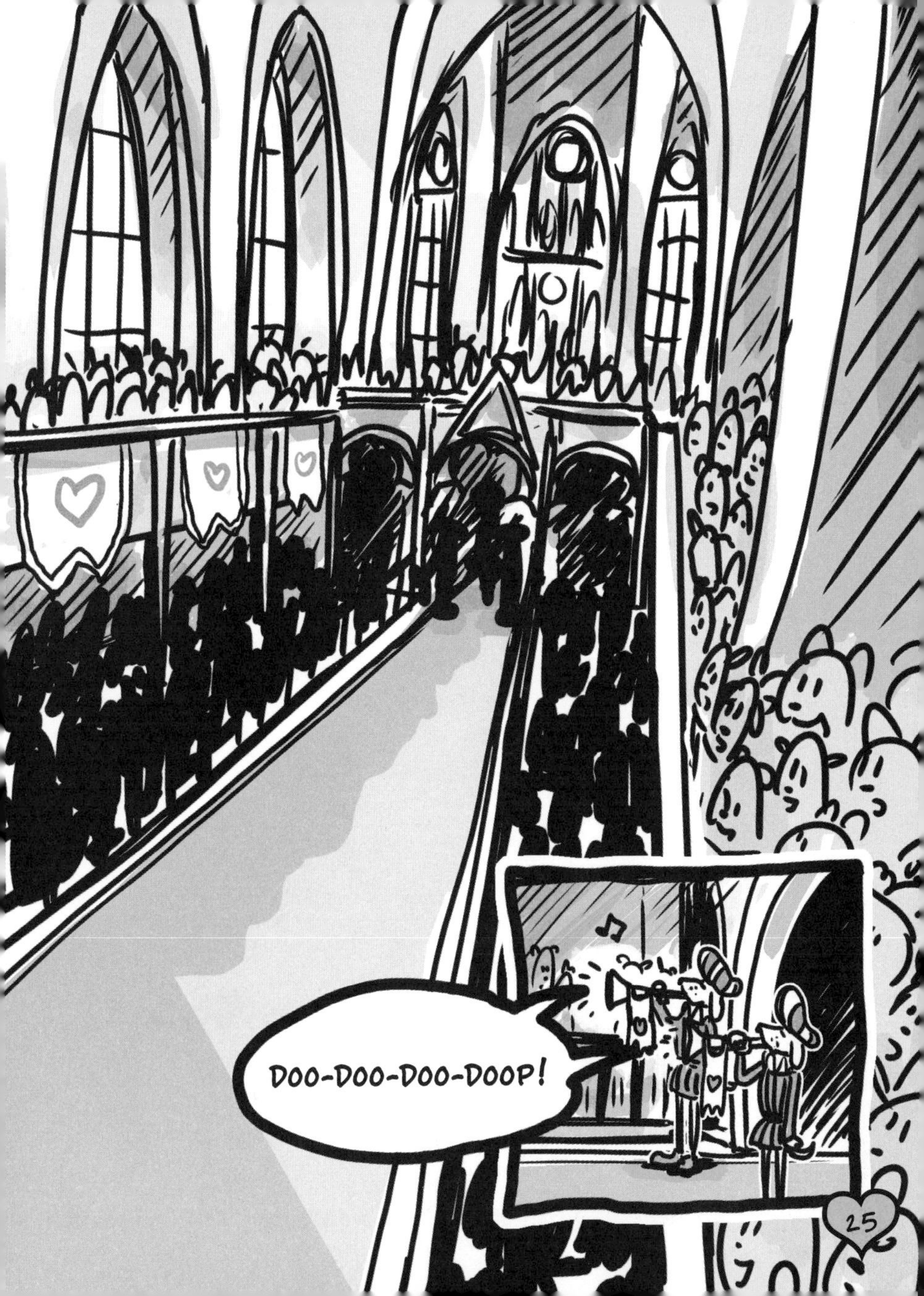
DOO-DOO-DOO-DOOP!

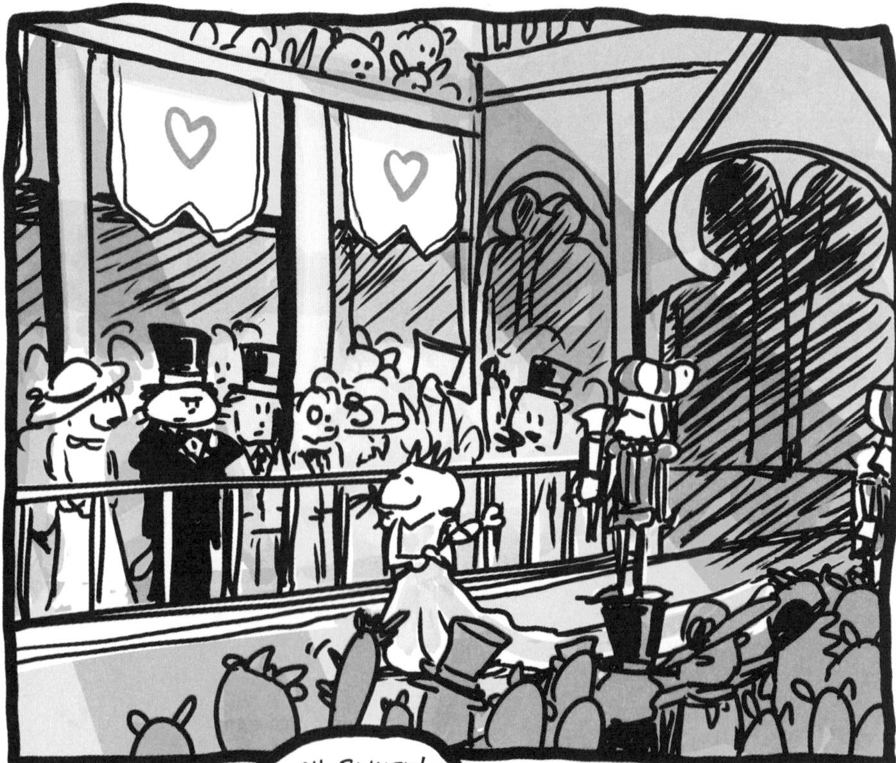

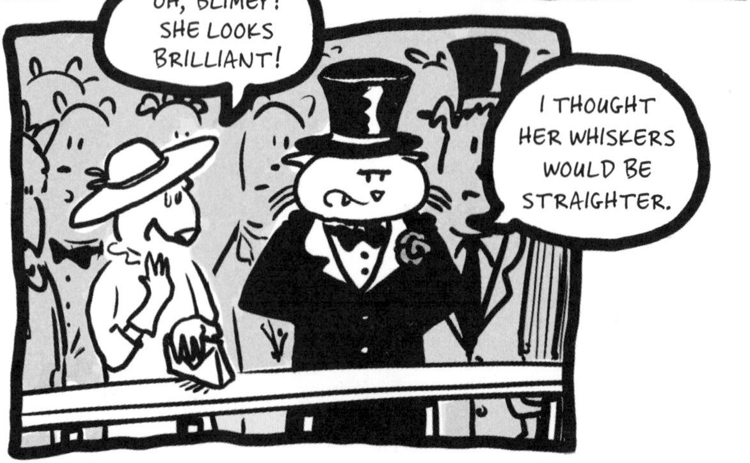
OH, BLIMEY! SHE LOOKS BRILLIANT!
I THOUGHT HER WHISKERS WOULD BE STRAIGHTER.

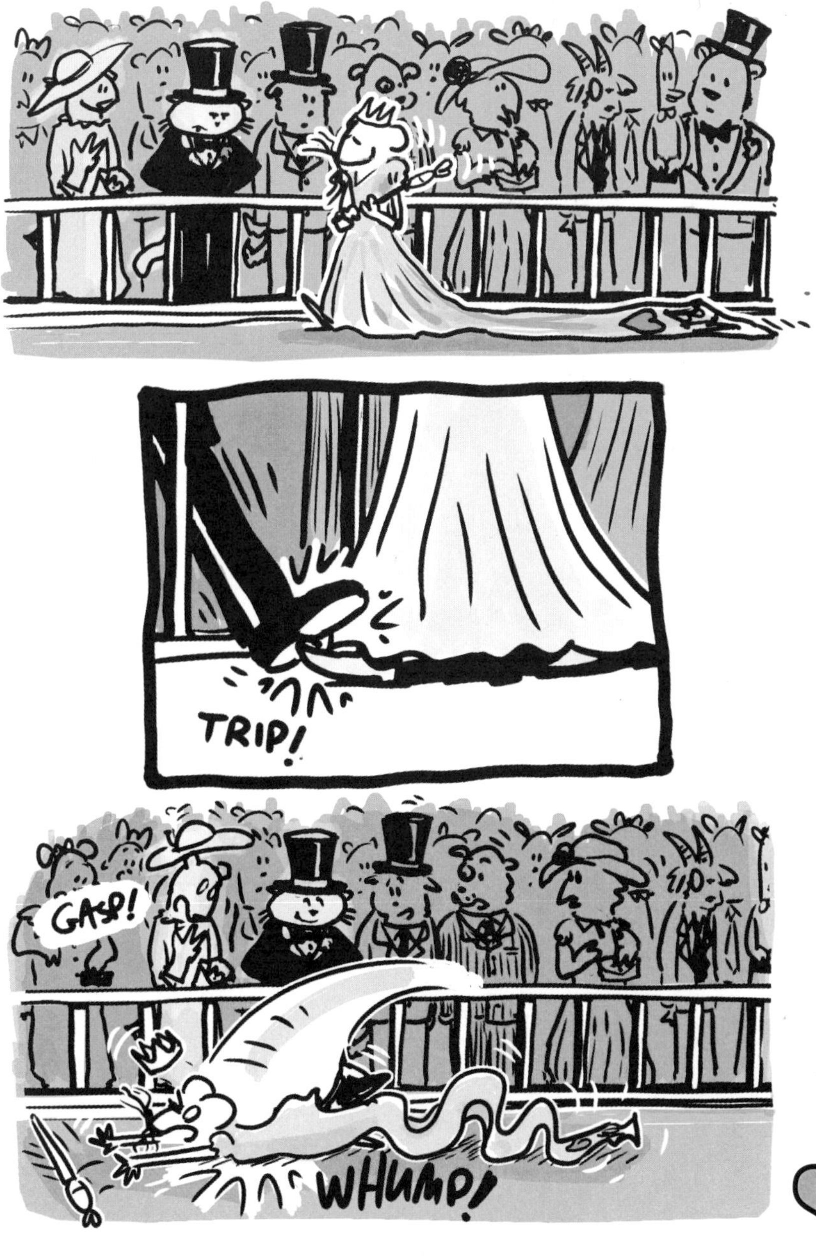
TRIP!
GASP!
WHUMP!

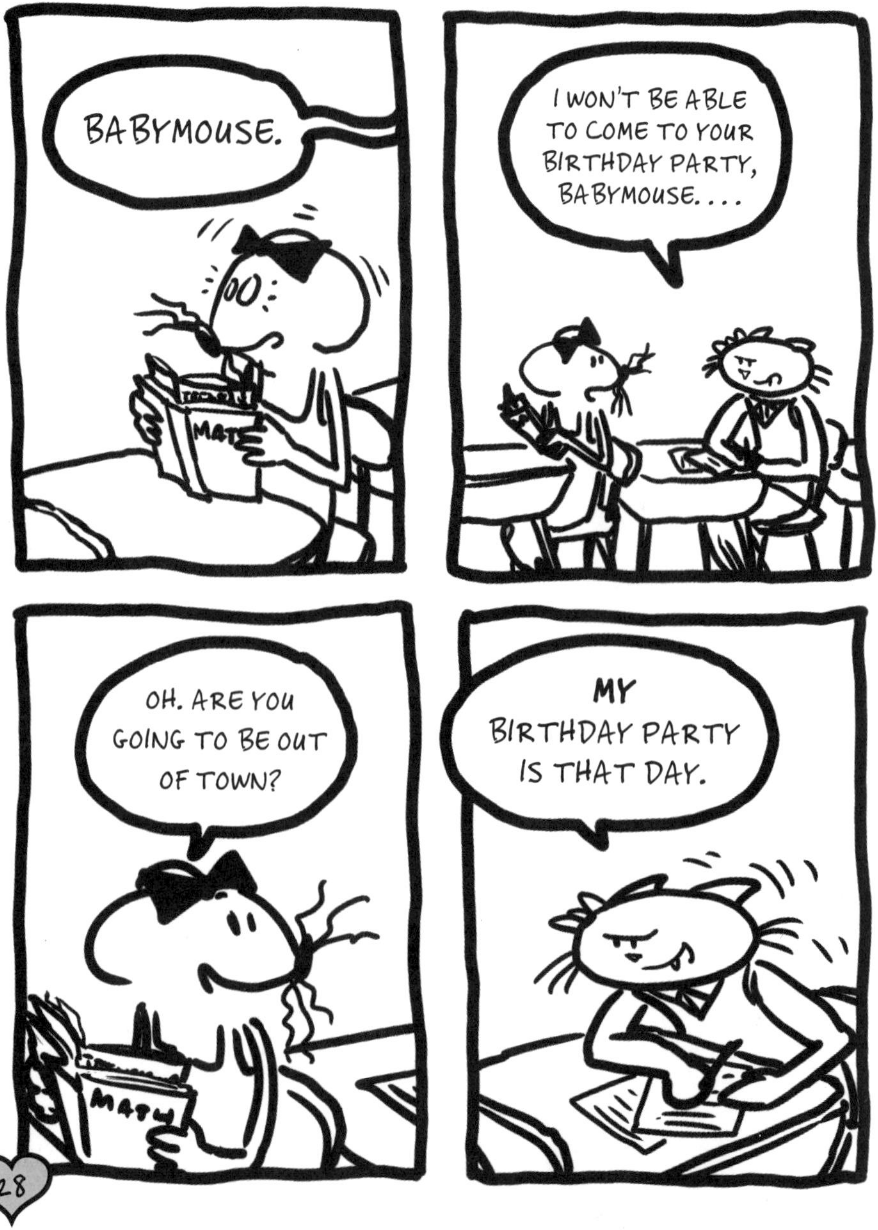
BABYMOUSE.
I WON'T BE ABLE TO COME TO YOUR BIRTHDAY PARTY, BABYMOUSE. . . .
OH. ARE YOU GOING TO BE OUT OF TOWN?
MY BIRTHDAY PARTY IS THAT DAY.

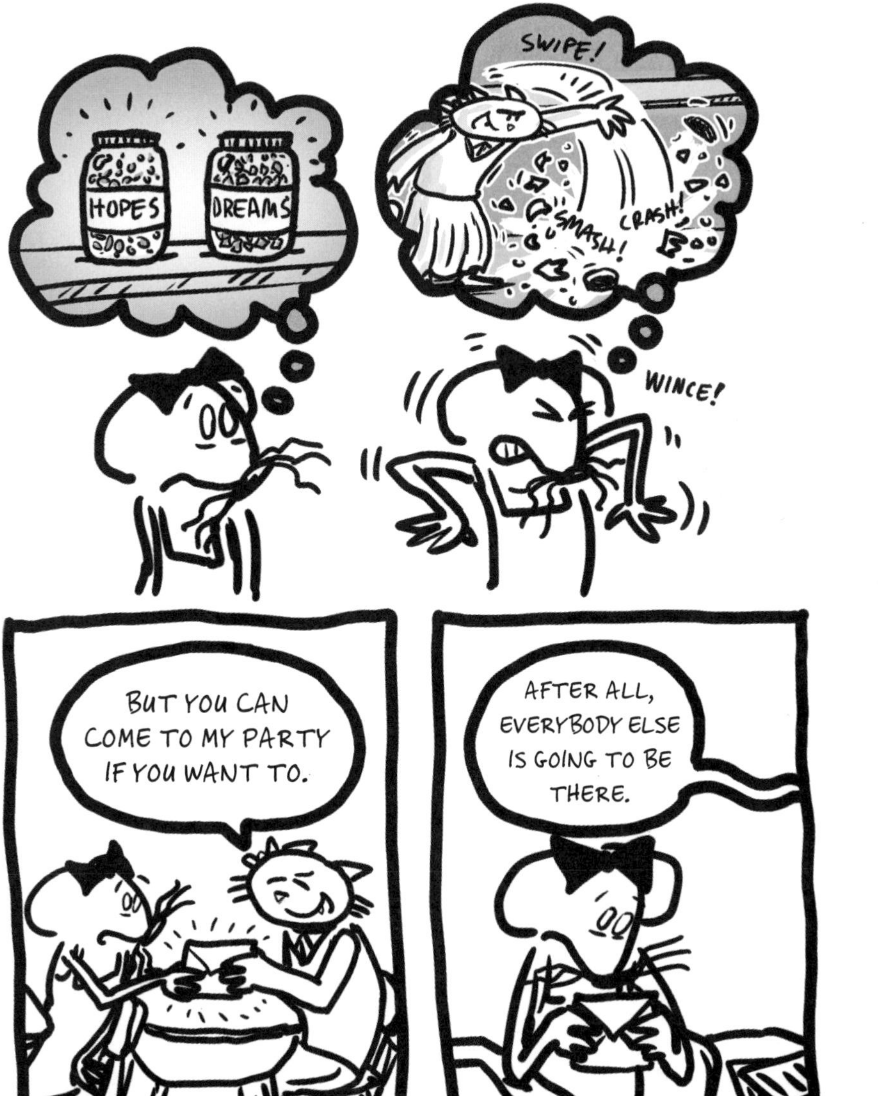
HOPES
DREAMS
SWIPE!
SMASH!
CRASH!
WINCE!
BUT YOU CAN COME TO MY PARTY IF YOU WANT TO.
AFTER ALL, EVERYBODY ELSE IS GOING TO BE THERE.

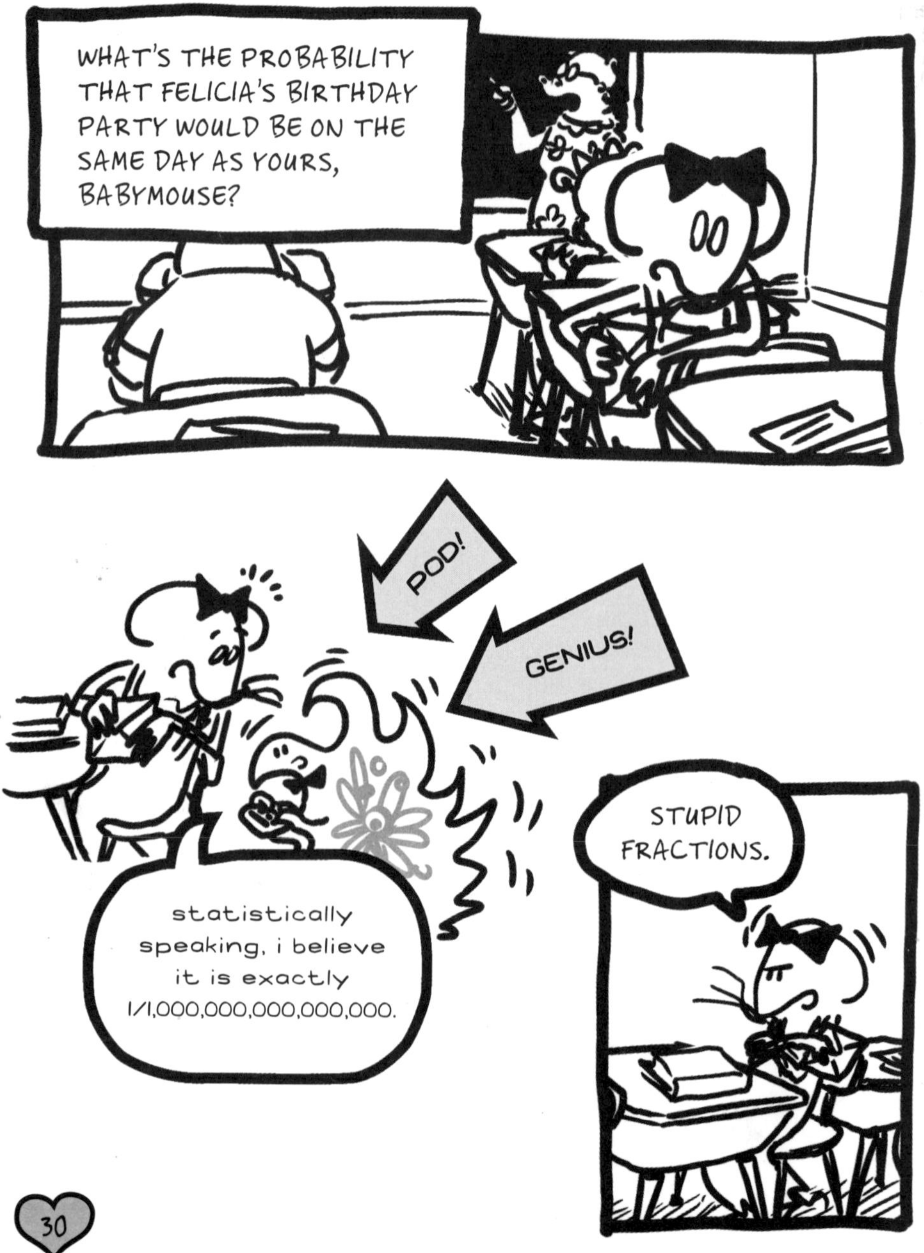
WHAT'S THE PROBABILITY THAT FELICIA'S BIRTHDAY PARTY WOULD BE ON THE SAME DAY AS YOURS, BABYMOUSE?
POD!
GENIUS!
statistically speaking, i believe it is exactly 1/1,000,000,000,000,000.
STUPID FRACTIONS.

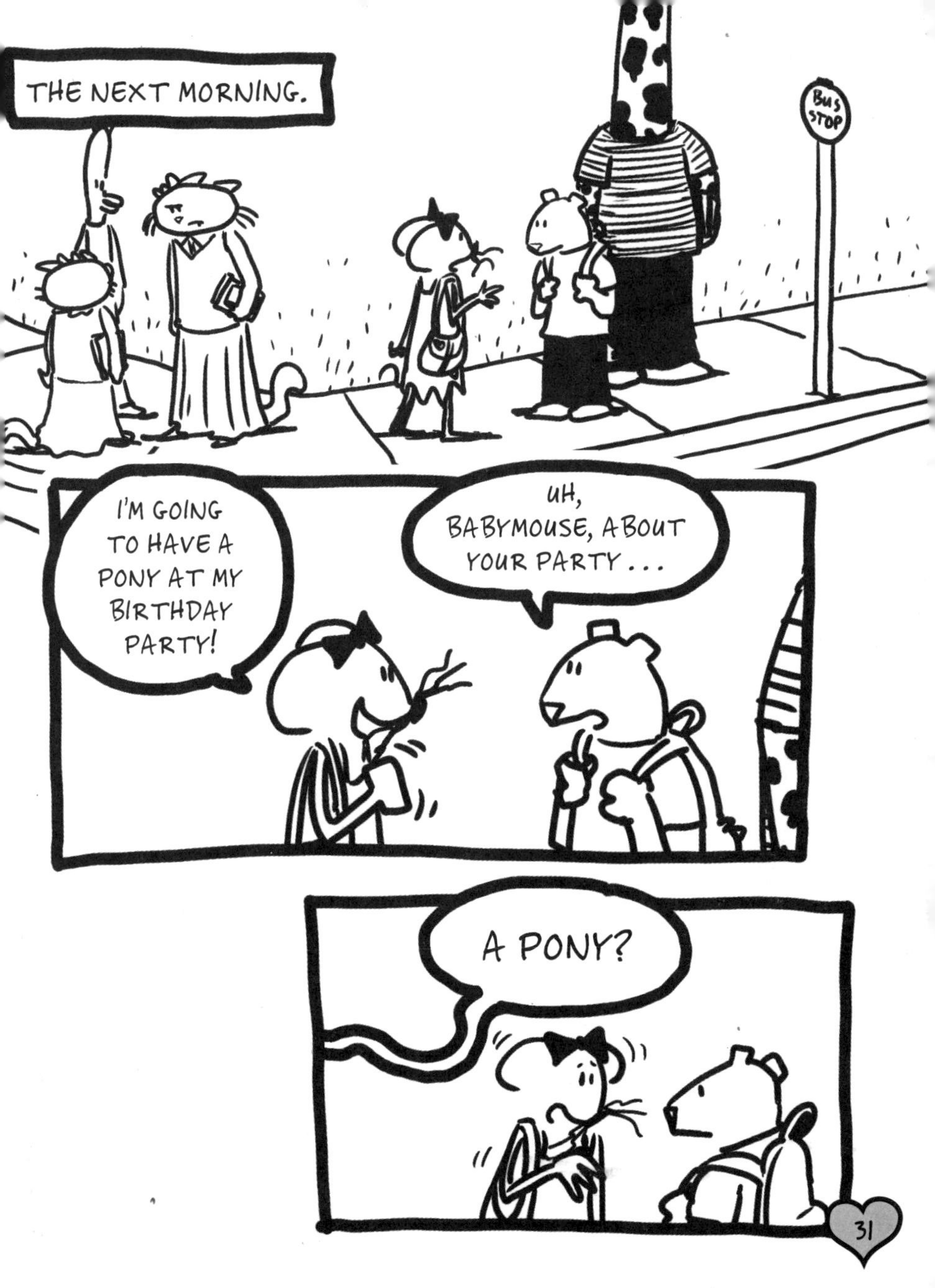
THE NEXT MORNING.
BUS STOP
I'M GOING TO HAVE A PONY AT MY BIRTHDAY PARTY!
UH, BABYMOUSE, ABOUT YOUR PARTY . . .
A PONY?

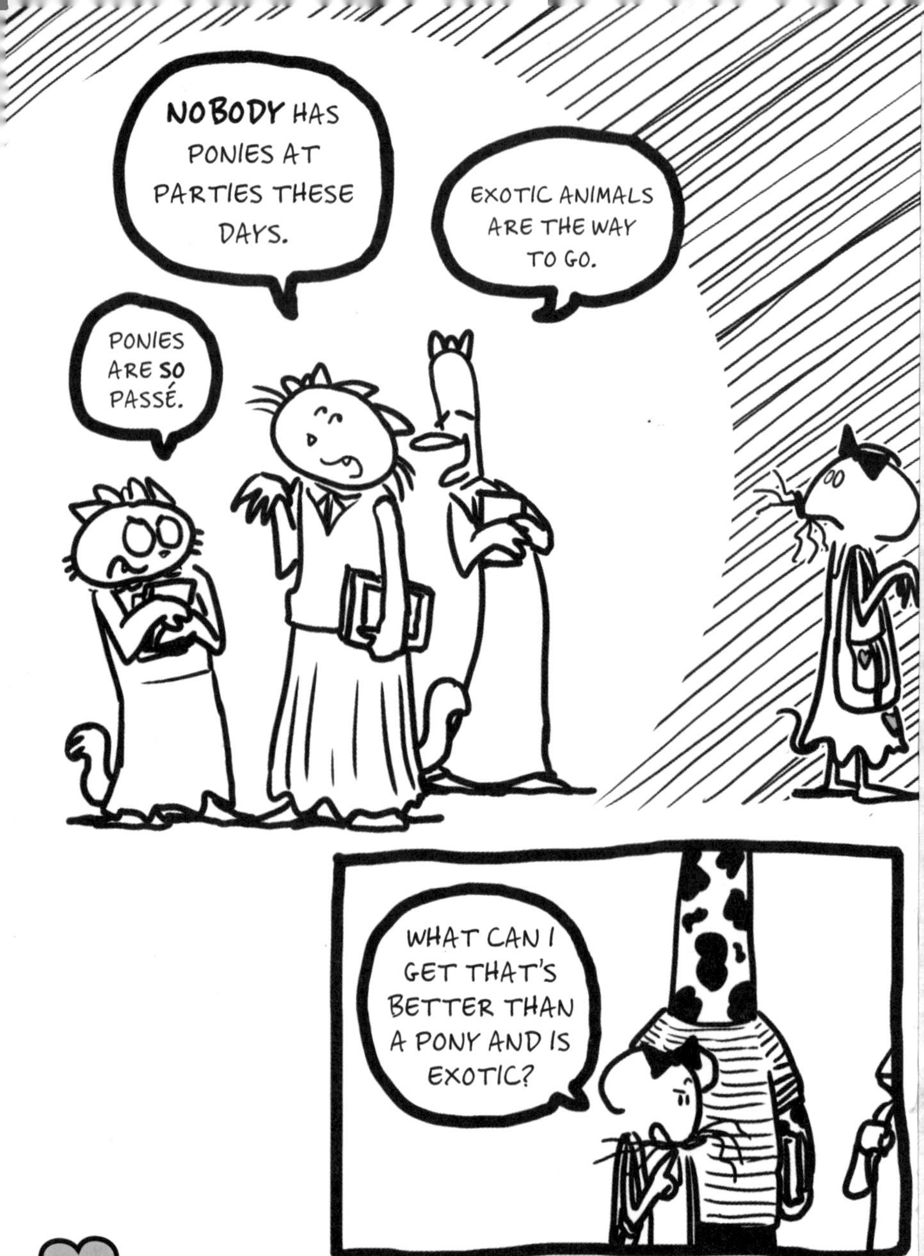
PONIES ARE SO PASSÉ.
NOBODY HAS PONIES AT PARTIES THESE DAYS.
EXOTIC ANIMALS ARE THE WAY TO GO.
WHAT CAN I GET THAT'S BETTER THAN A PONY AND IS EXOTIC?

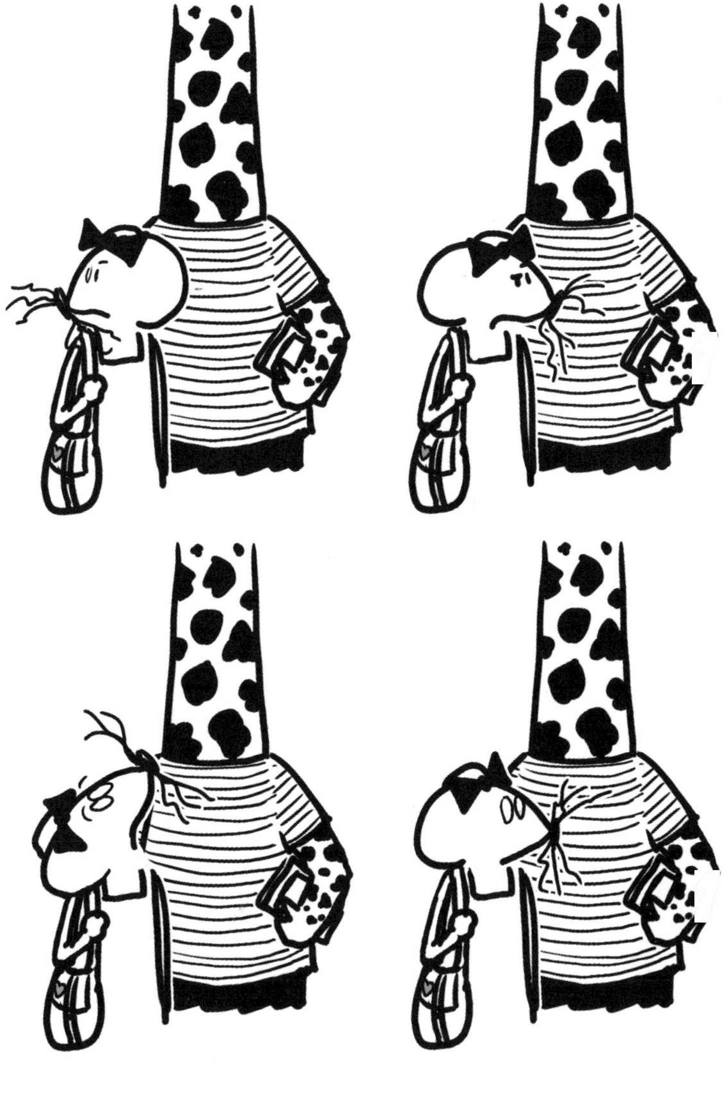

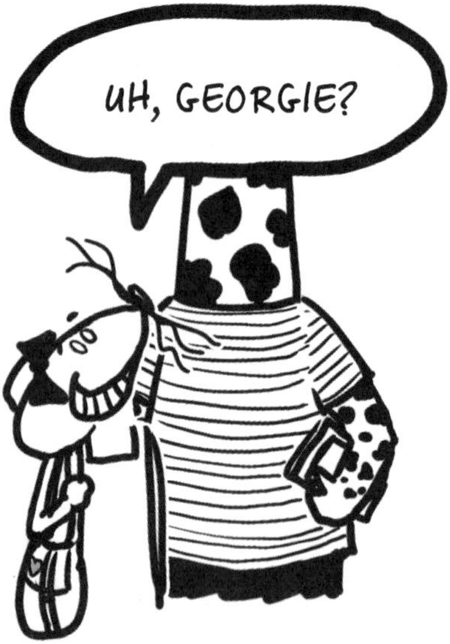
UH, GEORGIE?

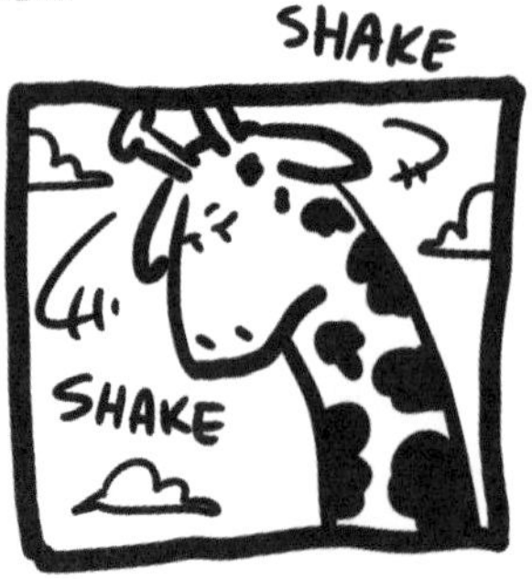
SHAKE
SHAKE

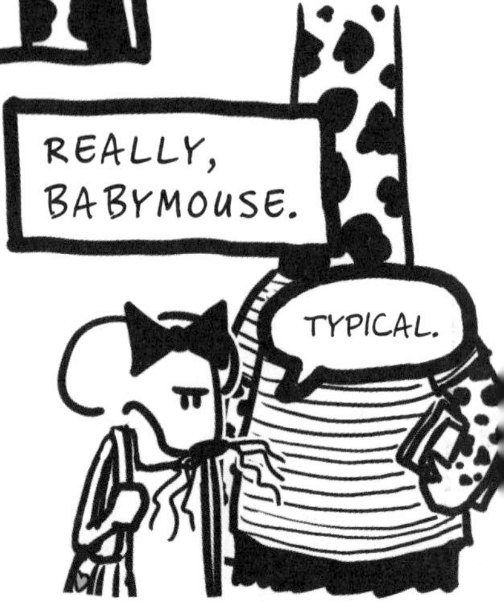
REALLY, BABYMOUSE.
TYPICAL.

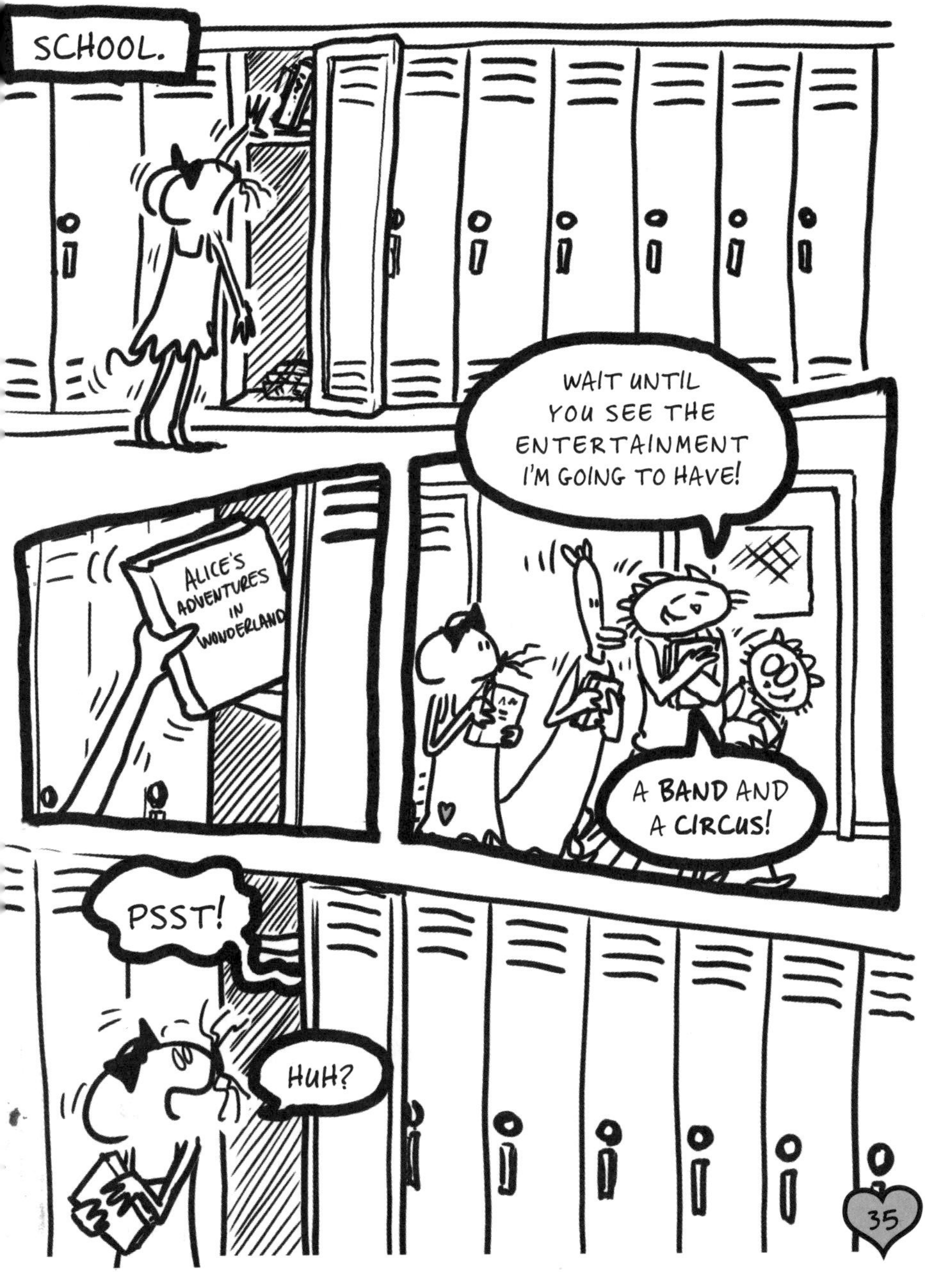
SCHOOL.
ALICE'S ADVENTURES IN WONDERLAND
WAIT UNTIL YOU SEE THE ENTERTAINMENT I'M GOING TO HAVE!
A BAND AND A CIRCUS!
PSST!
HUH?

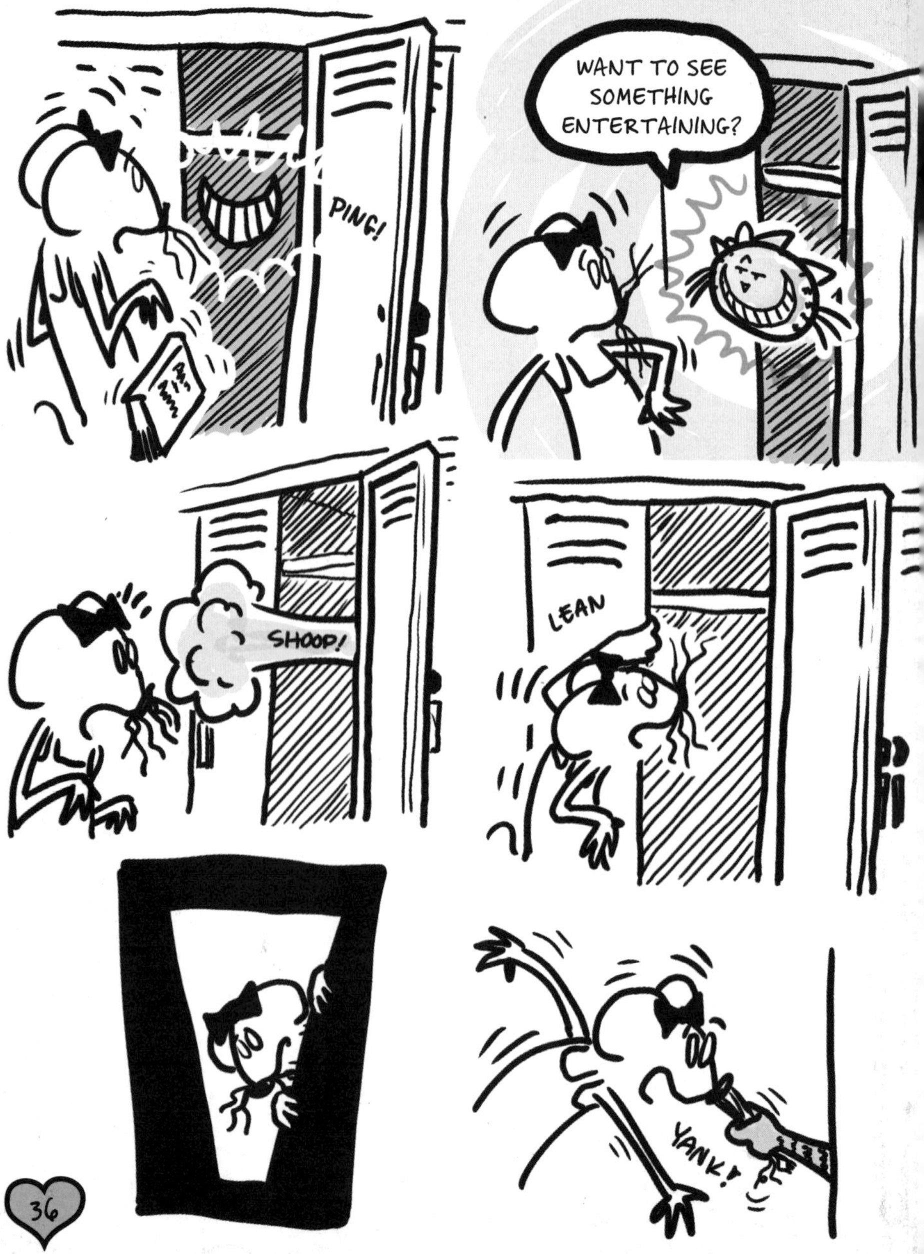
PING!
WANT TO SEE SOMETHING ENTERTAINING?
SHOOP!
LEAN
YANK!

HA!
HEEEYYYYYYY!!!

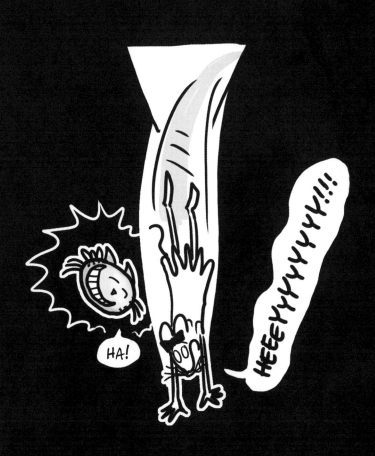

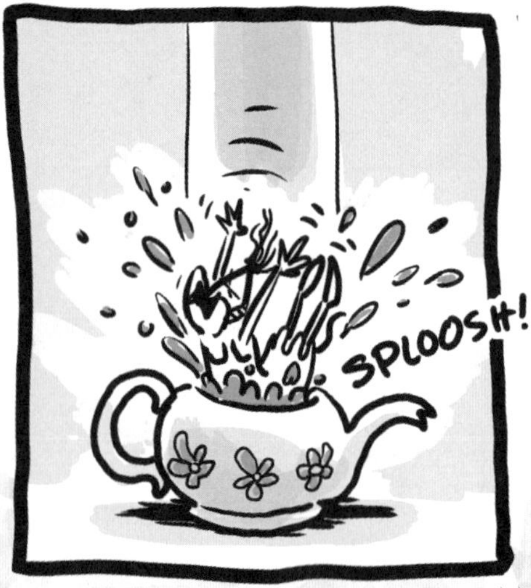
SPLOOSH!

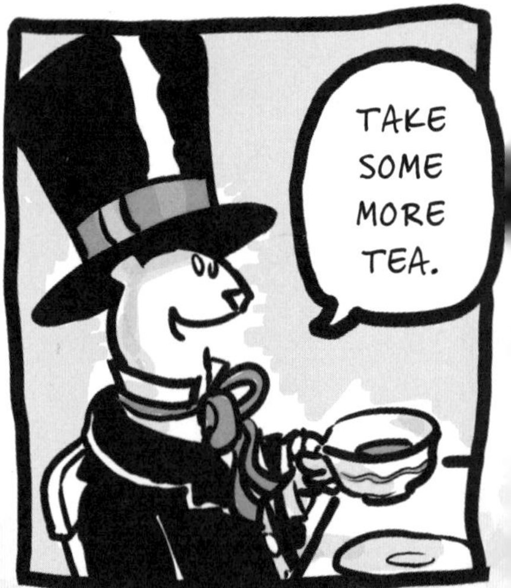
TAKE SOME MORE TEA.

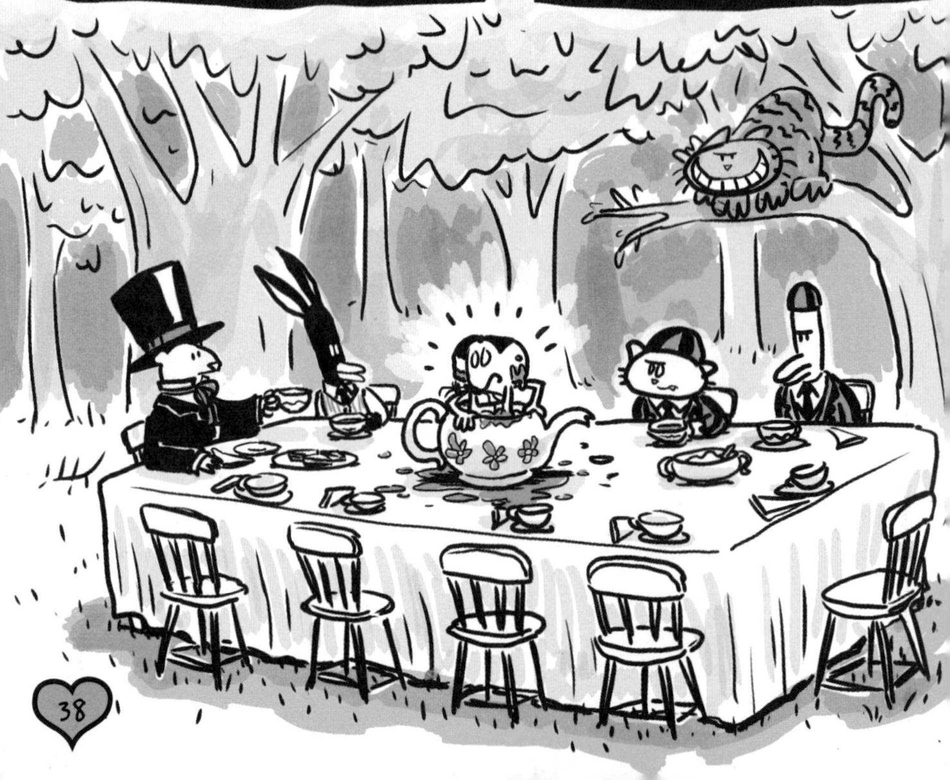

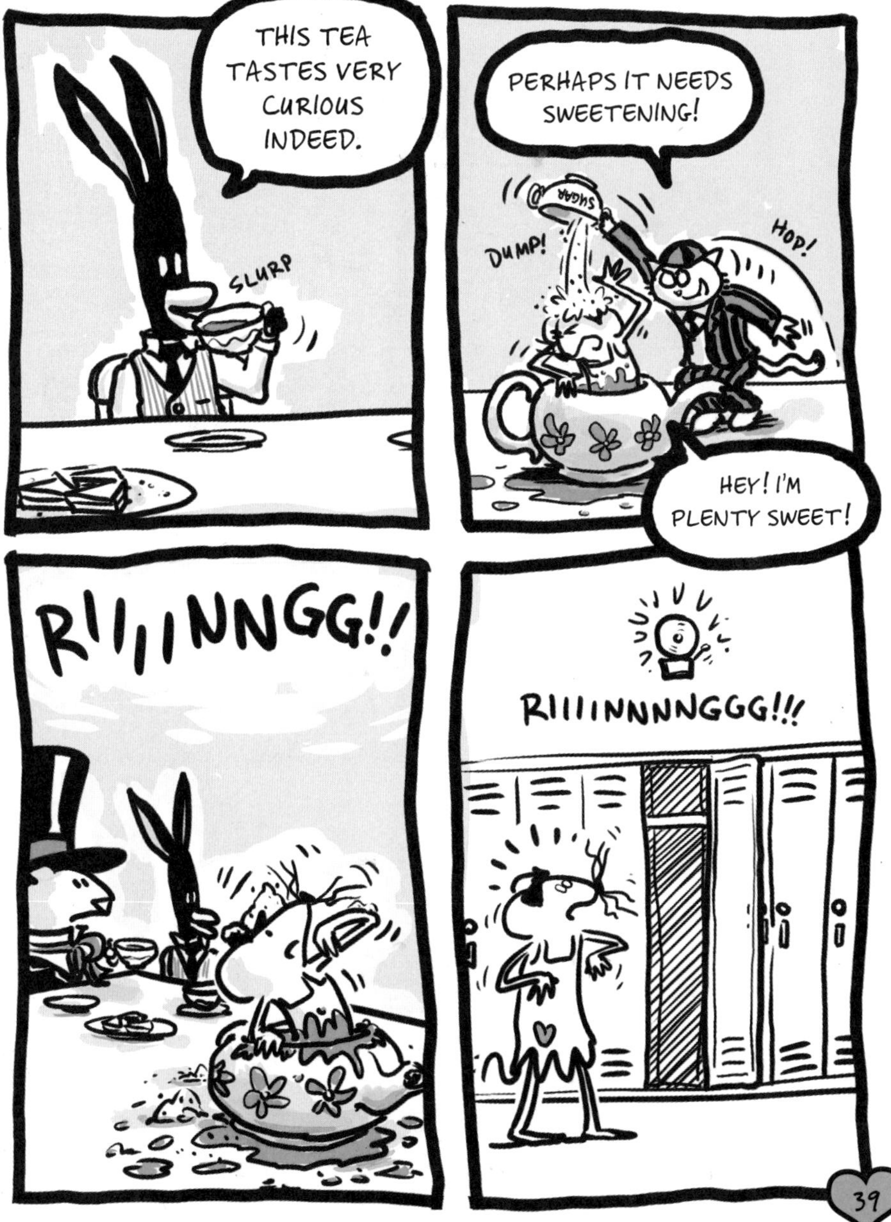
THIS TEA TASTES VERY CURIOUS INDEED.
SLURP
PERHAPS IT NEEDS SWEETENING!
SUGAR
DUMP!
HOP!
HEY! I'M PLENTY SWEET!
RIIIINNGG!!
RIIIINNNNGGG!!!

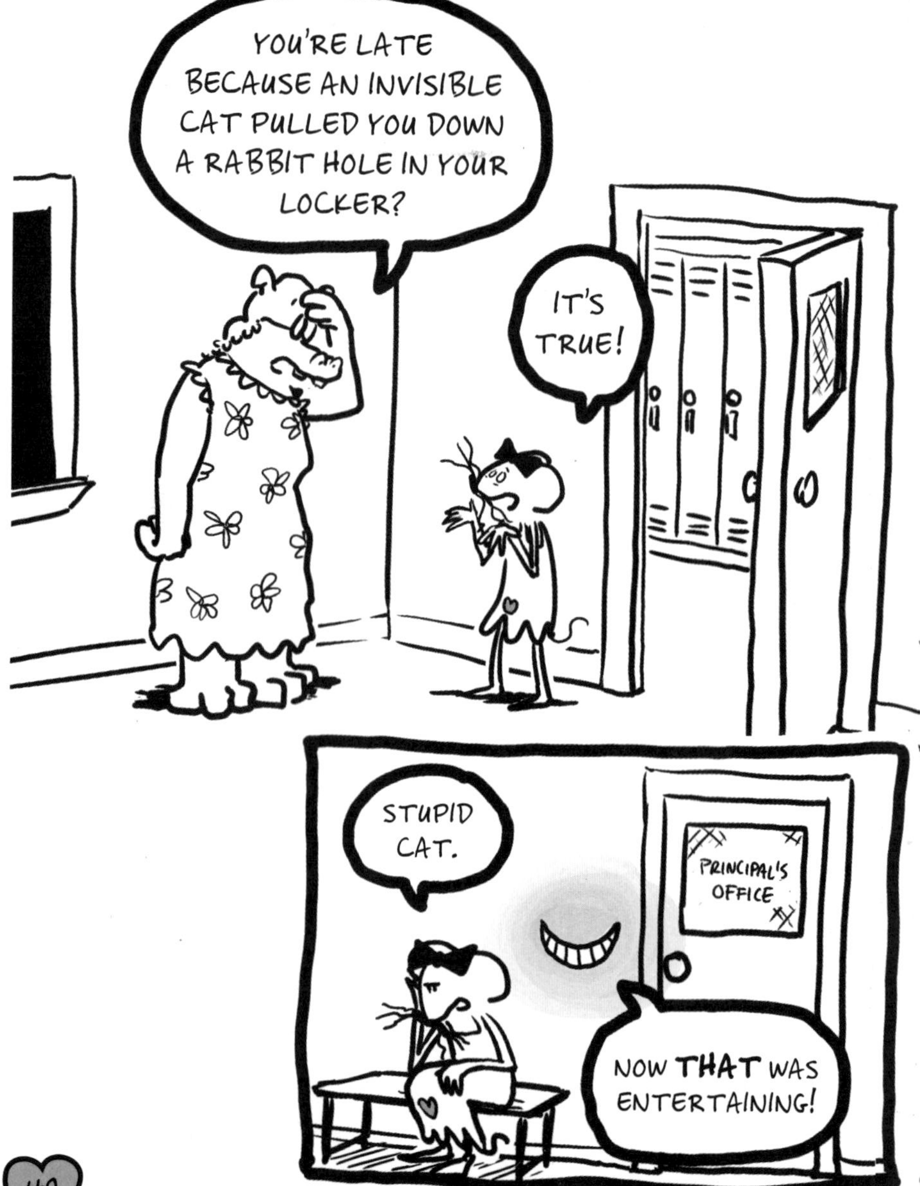
YOU'RE LATE BECAUSE AN INVISIBLE CAT PULLED YOU DOWN A RABBIT HOLE IN YOUR LOCKER?
IT'S TRUE!
STUPID CAT.
PRINCIPAL'S OFFICE
NOW **THAT** WAS ENTERTAINING!

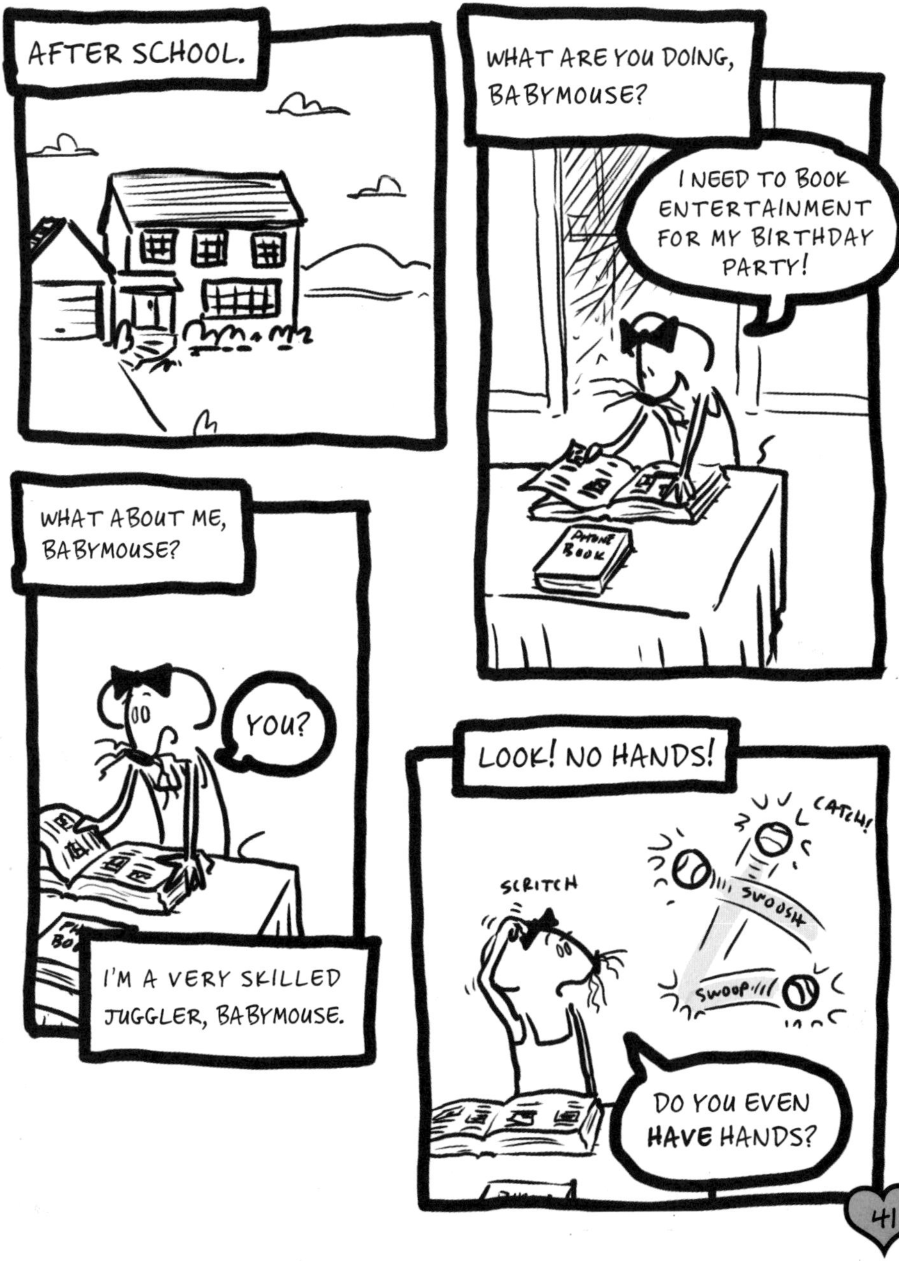

AFTER SCHOOL.
WHAT ARE YOU DOING, BABYMOUSE?
I NEED TO BOOK ENTERTAINMENT FOR MY BIRTHDAY PARTY!
PHONE BOOK
WHAT ABOUT ME, BABYMOUSE?
YOU?
I'M A VERY SKILLED JUGGLER, BABYMOUSE.
LOOK! NO HANDS!
CATCH!
SCRITCH
SWOOSH
SWOOP
DO YOU EVEN HAVE HANDS?

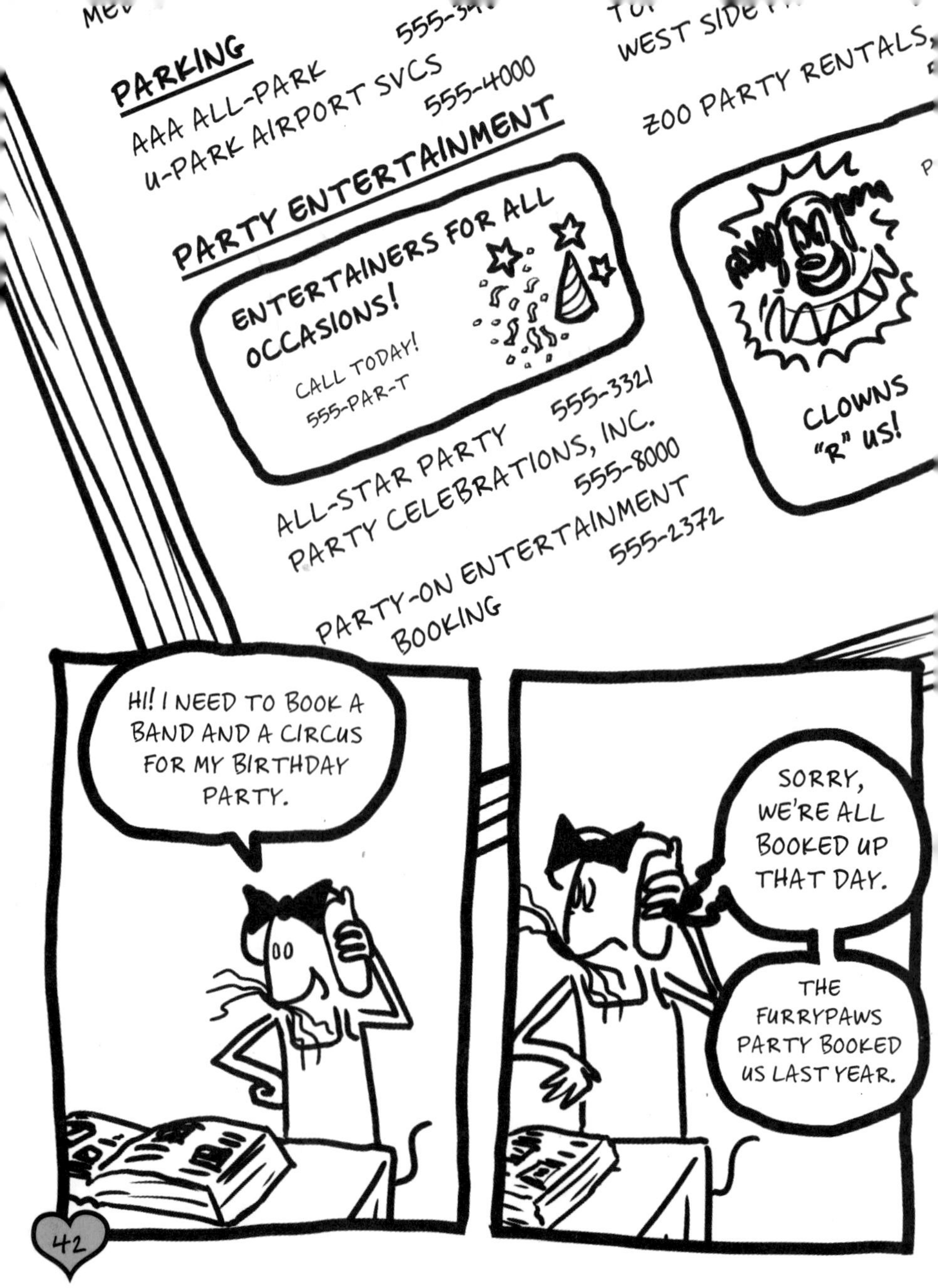

PARKING
AAA ALL-PARK
U-PARK AIRPORT SVCS 555-4000
WEST SIDE
PARTY RENTALS,
ZOO PARTY RENTALS
PARTY ENTERTAINMENT
ENTERTAINERS FOR ALL OCCASIONS!
CALL TODAY! 555-PAR-T
CLOWNS "R" US!
ALL-STAR PARTY 555-3321
PARTY CELEBRATIONS, INC. 555-8000
PARTY-ON ENTERTAINMENT 555-2372
PARTY-ON BOOKING
HI! I NEED TO BOOK A BAND AND A CIRCUS FOR MY BIRTHDAY PARTY.
SORRY, WE'RE ALL BOOKED UP THAT DAY.
THE FURRYPAWS PARTY BOOKED US LAST YEAR.

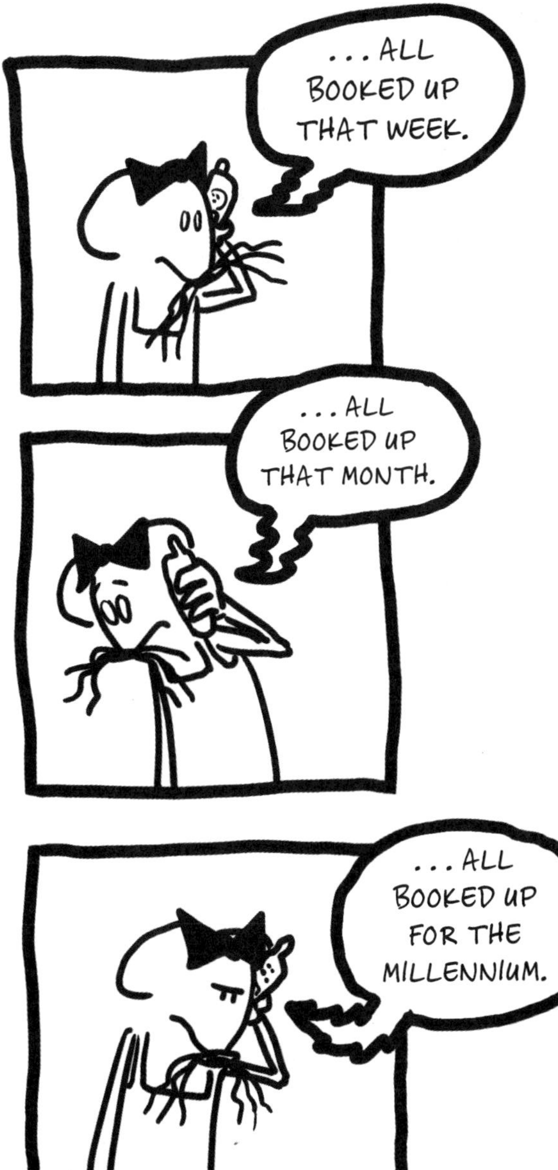
...ALL BOOKED UP THAT WEEK.
...ALL BOOKED UP THAT MONTH.
...ALL BOOKED UP FOR THE MILLENNIUM.

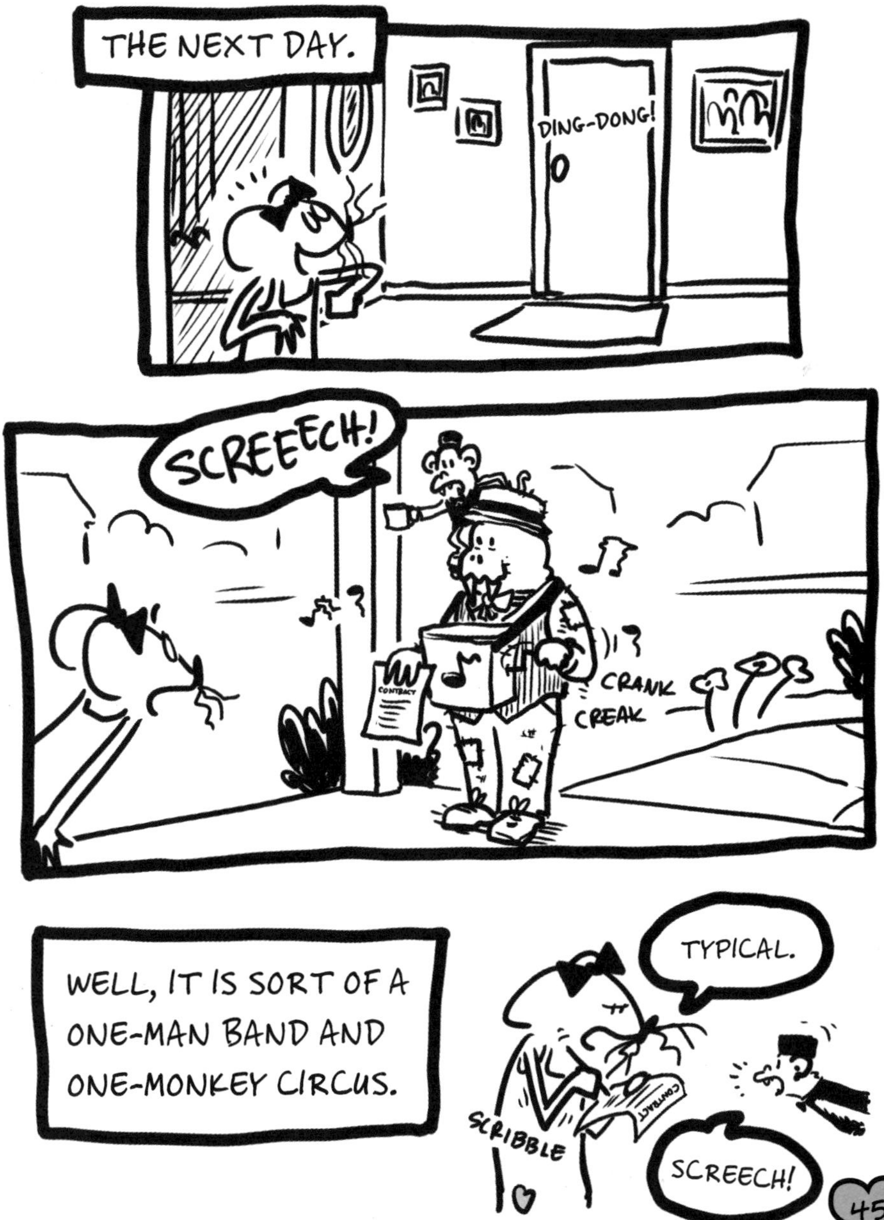

THE NEXT DAY.
DING-DONG!
SCREEECH!
CONTRACT
CRANK
CREAK
WELL, IT IS SORT OF A ONE-MAN BAND AND ONE-MONKEY CIRCUS.
TYPICAL.
CONTRACT
SCRIBBLE
SCREECH!

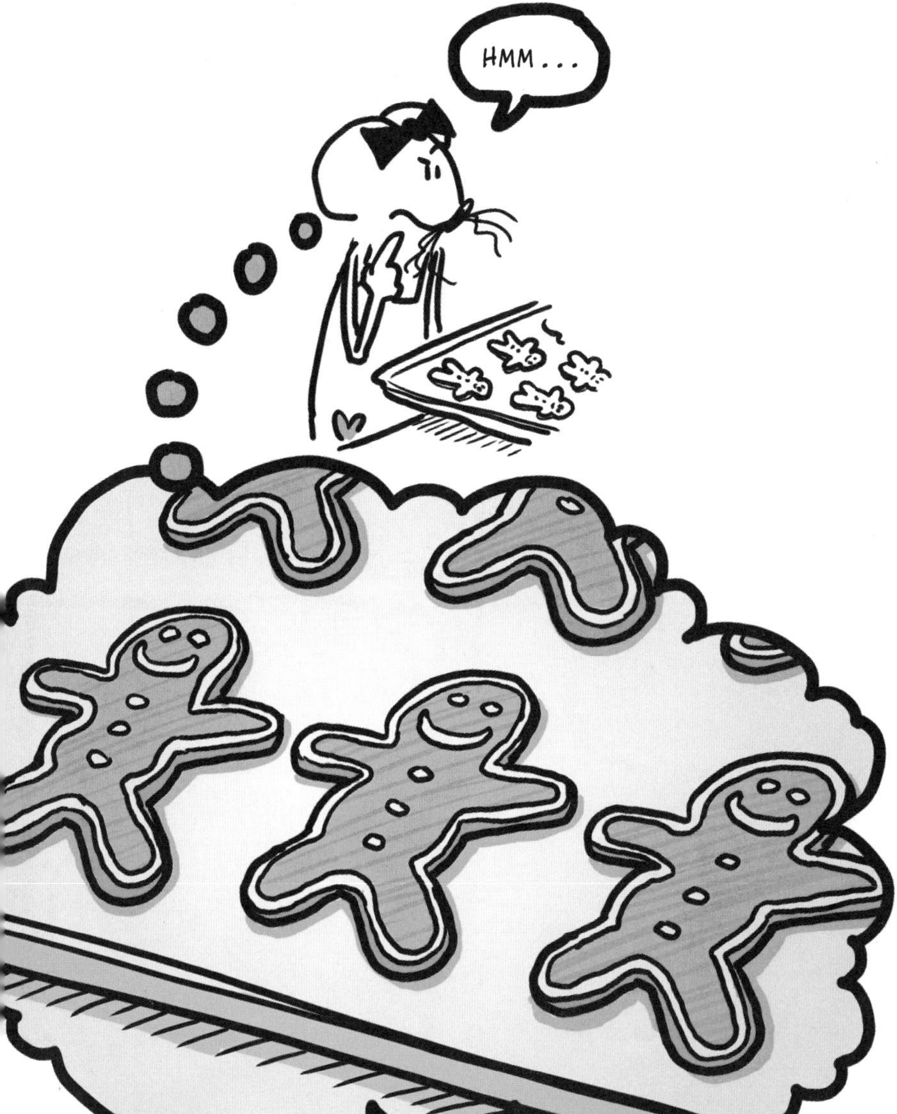
HMM . . .

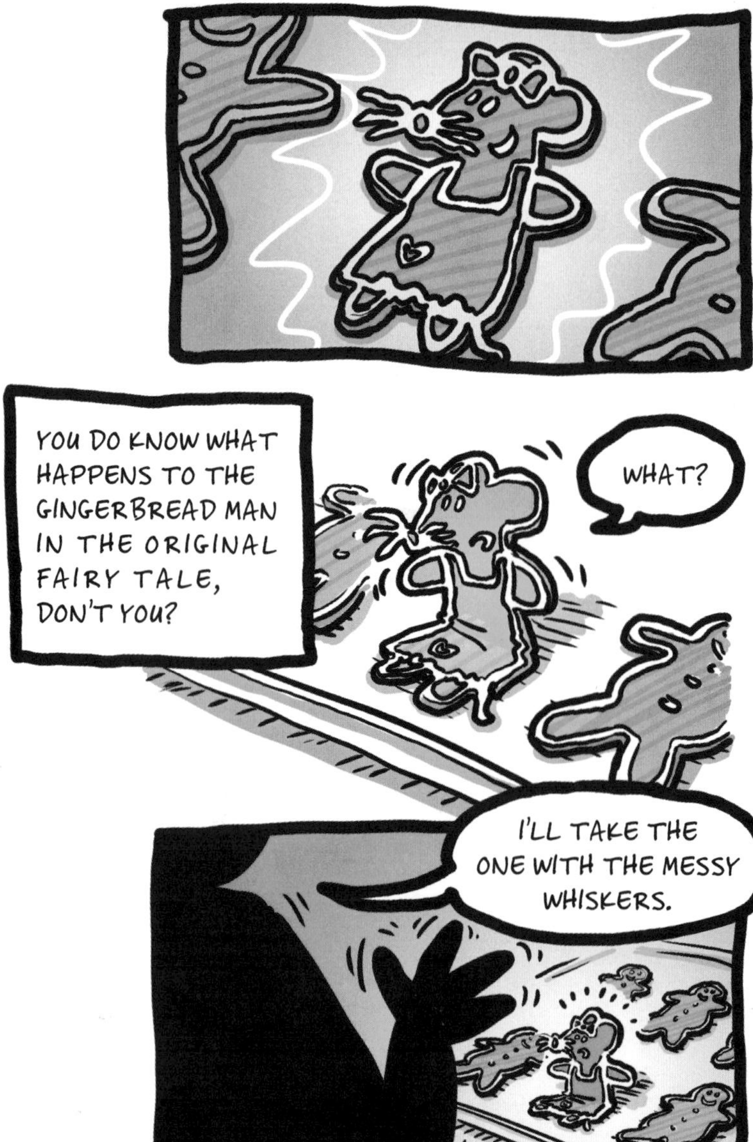
YOU DO KNOW WHAT HAPPENS TO THE GINGERBREAD MAN IN THE ORIGINAL FAIRY TALE, DON'T YOU?
WHAT?
I'LL TAKE THE ONE WITH THE MESSY WHISKERS.

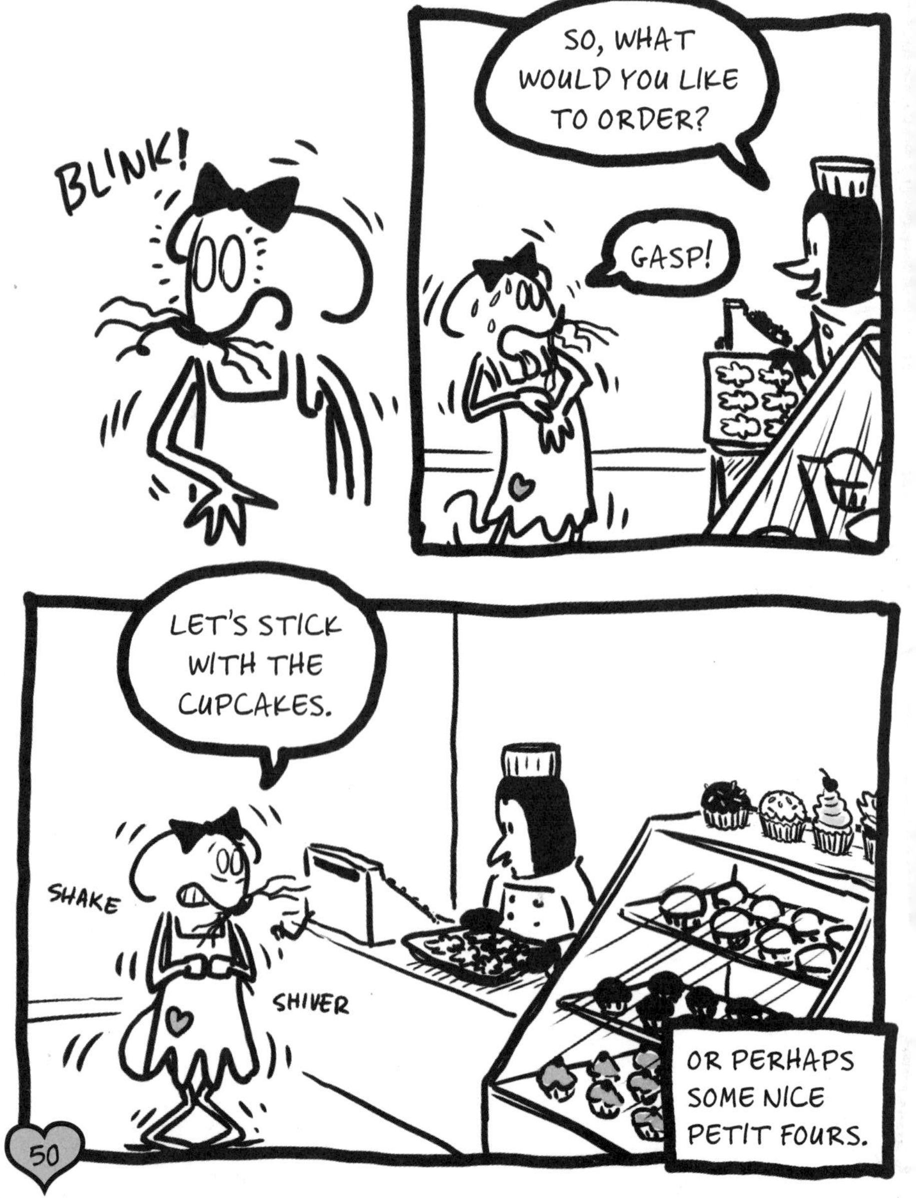
BLINK!
SO, WHAT WOULD YOU LIKE TO ORDER?
GASP!
LET'S STICK WITH THE CUPCAKES.
SHAKE
SHIVER
OR PERHAPS SOME NICE PETIT FOURS.

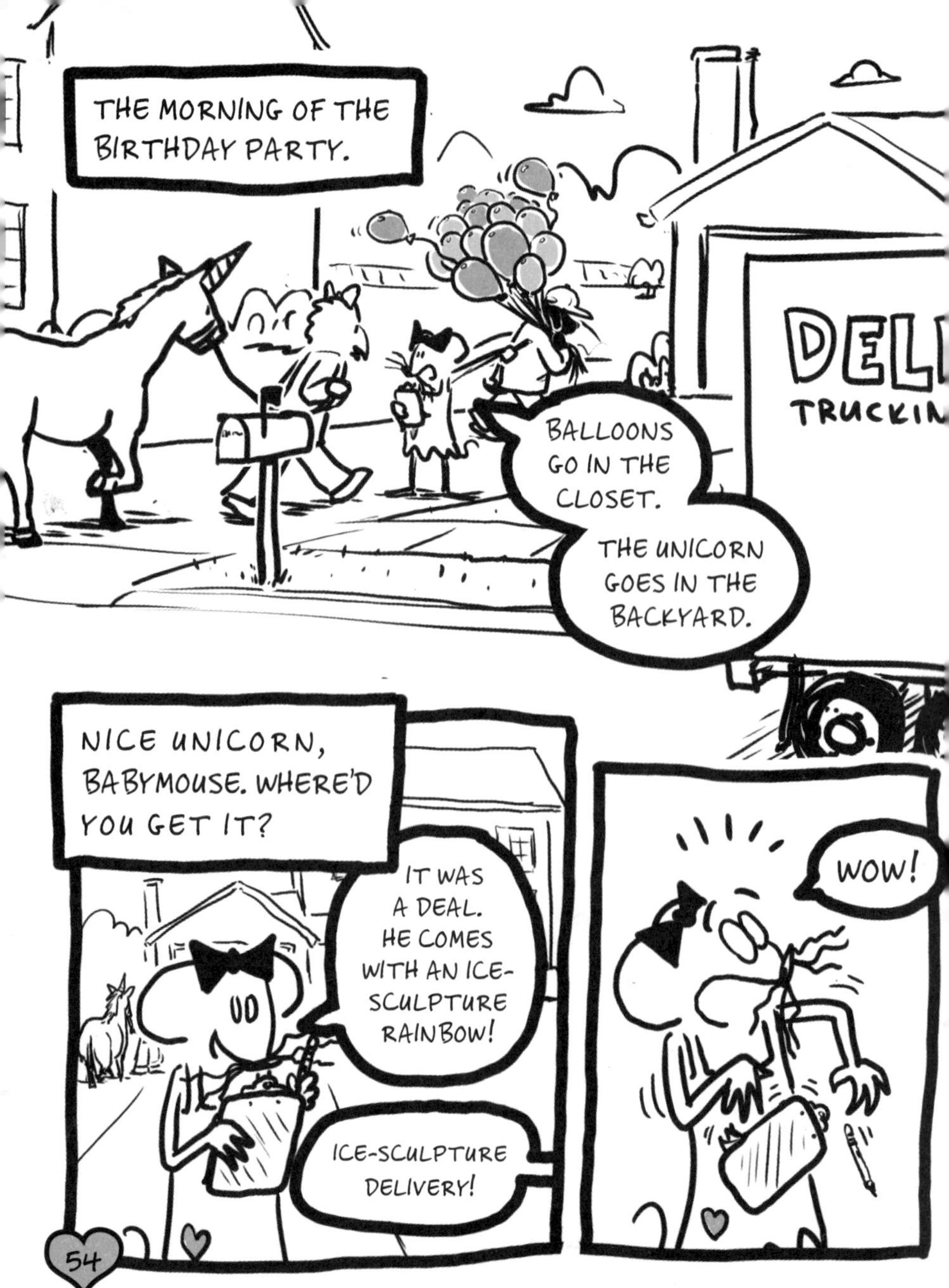
THE MORNING OF THE BIRTHDAY PARTY.
DEL
TRUCKIN
BALLOONS GO IN THE CLOSET.
THE UNICORN GOES IN THE BACKYARD.
NICE UNICORN, BABYMOUSE. WHERE'D YOU GET IT?
IT WAS A DEAL. HE COMES WITH AN ICE-SCULPTURE RAINBOW!
ICE-SCULPTURE DELIVERY!
WOW!

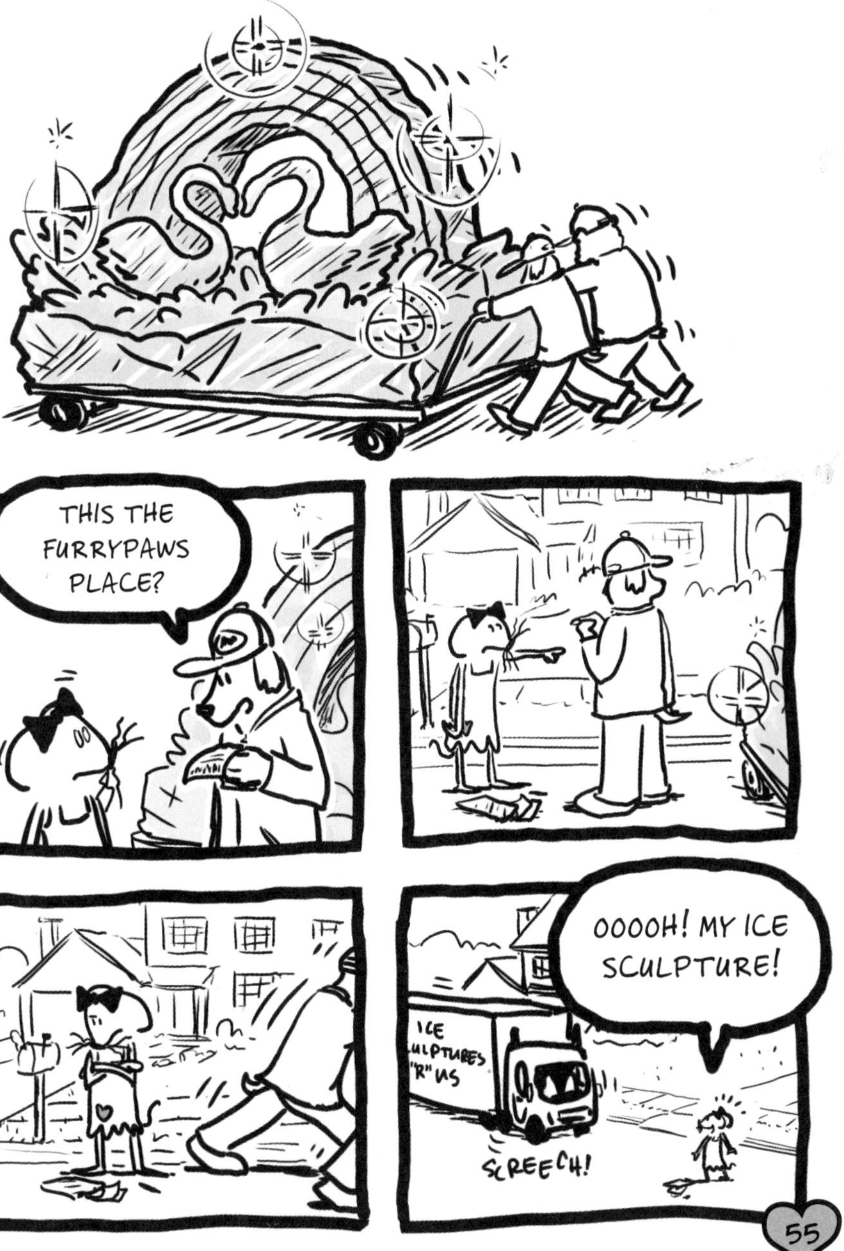
THIS THE FURRYPAWS PLACE?
OOOOH! MY ICE SCULPTURE!
ICE
ULPTURES
"R" US
SCREECH!

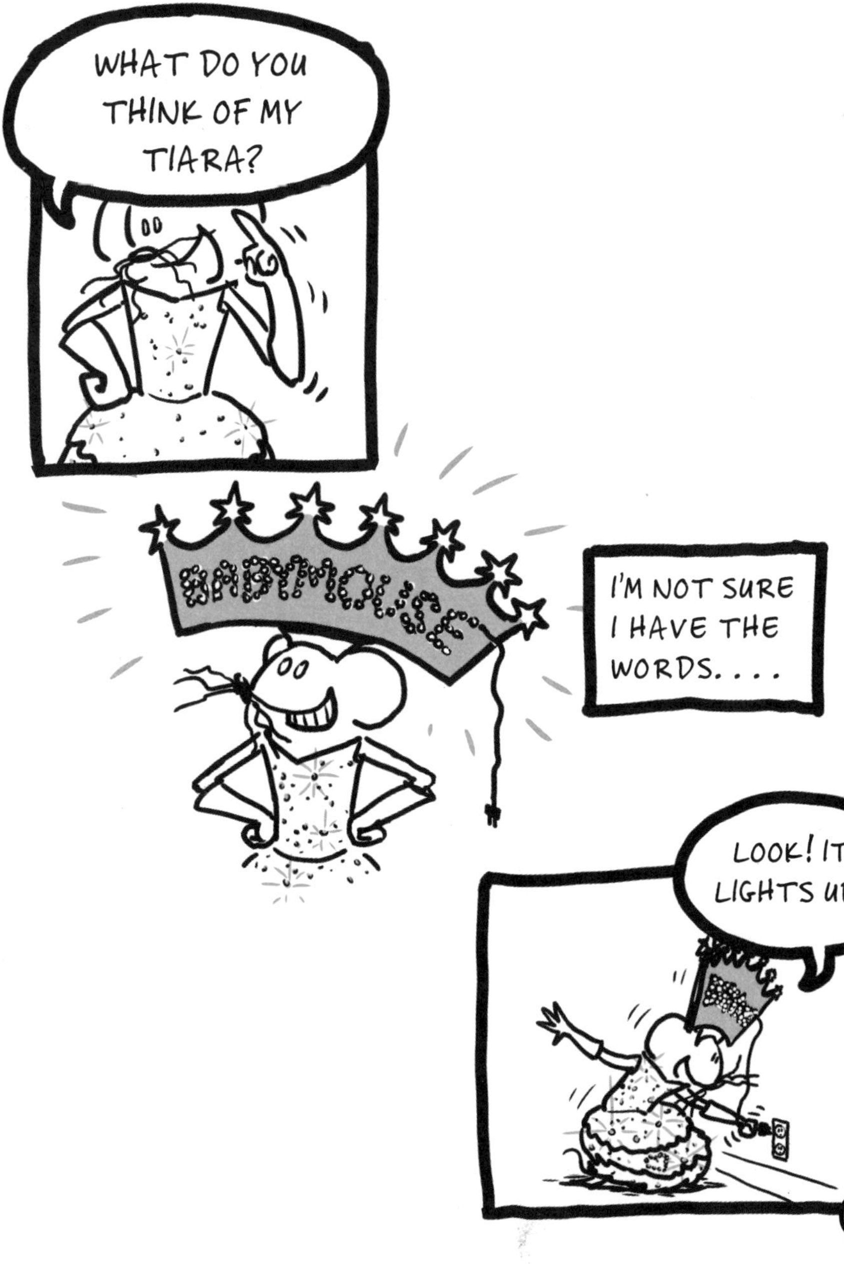
WHAT DO YOU THINK OF MY TIARA?
BABYMOUSE
I'M NOT SURE I HAVE THE WORDS. . . .
LOOK! IT LIGHTS UP!

ZZZZZAAAPPP!

BABYMOUSE

THE WORDS I WAS SEARCHING FOR WOULD BE "ABSOLUTELY ELECTRIFYING."

EEP.

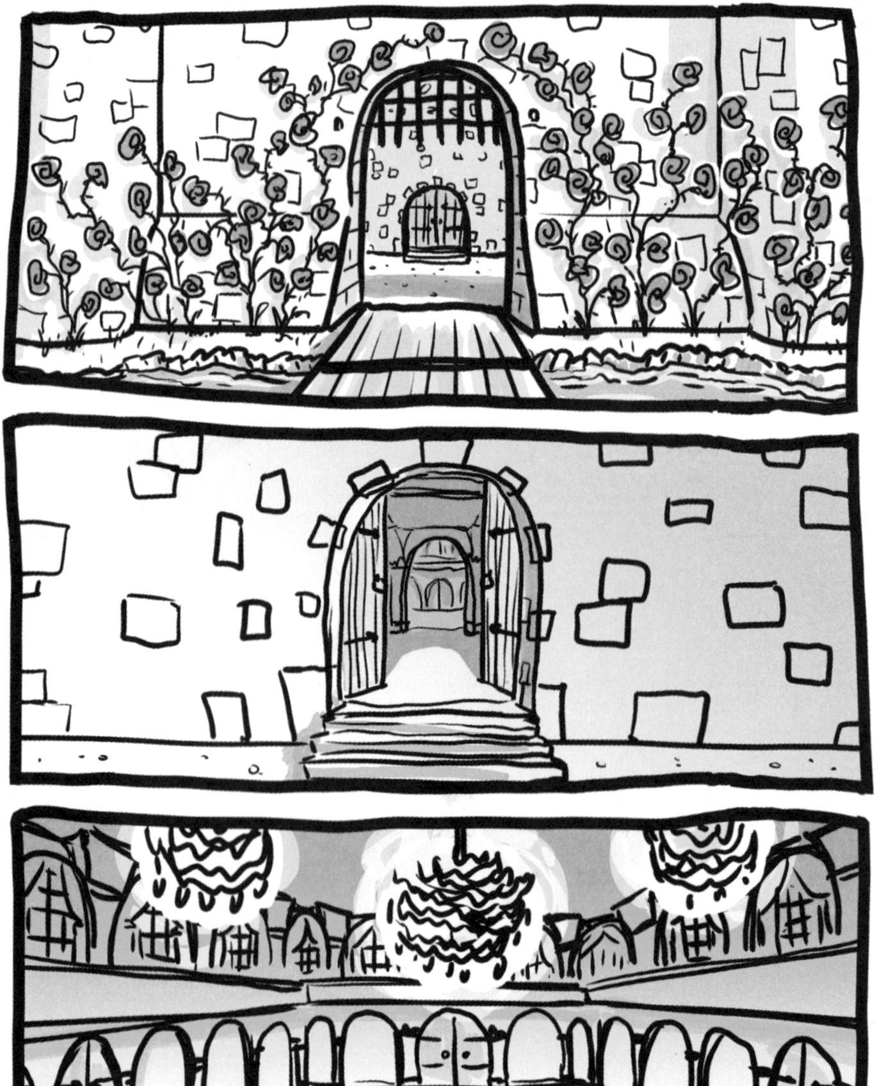

PARTY TIME.
TICK
TOCK
TICK
TOCK
TICK
TOCK
TICK
TOCK

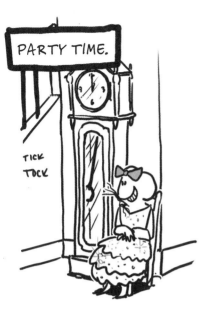

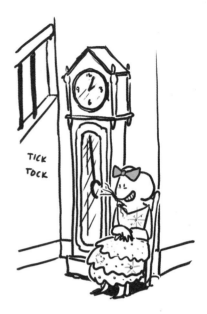

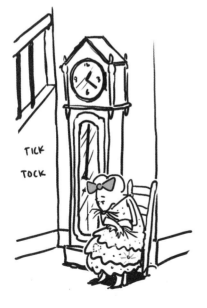

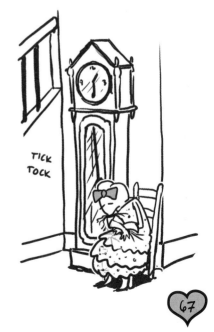

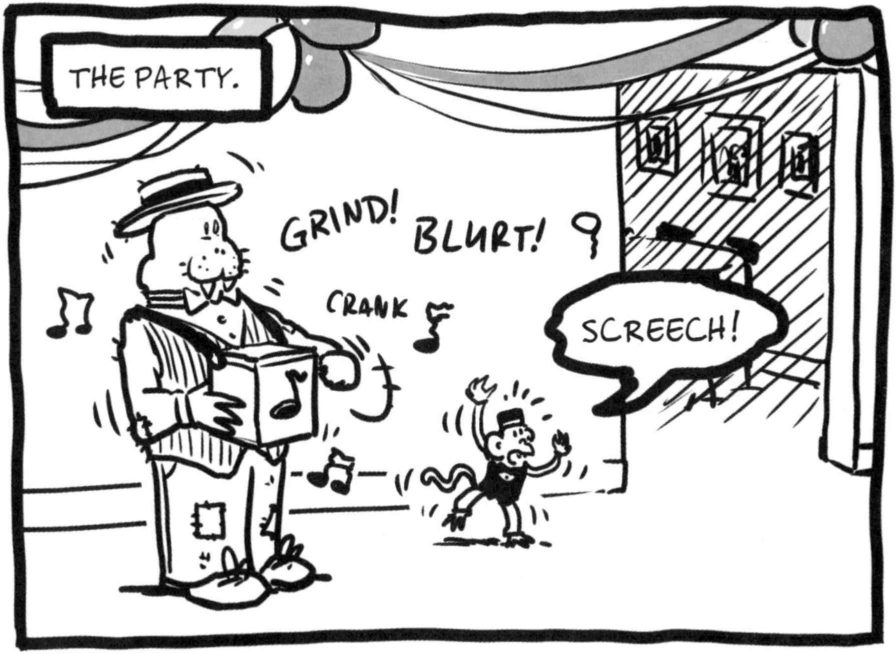
THE PARTY.
GRIND!
BLURT!
CRANK
SCREECH!

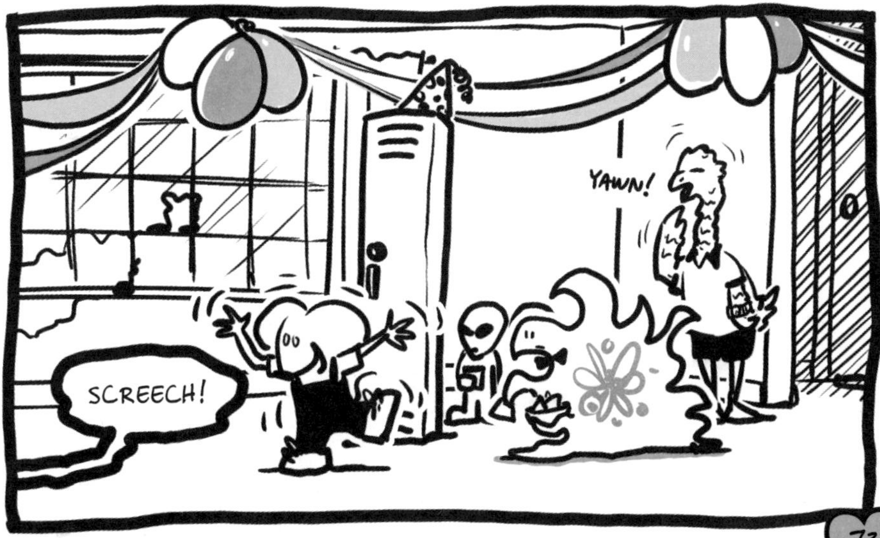
YAWN!
SCREECH!

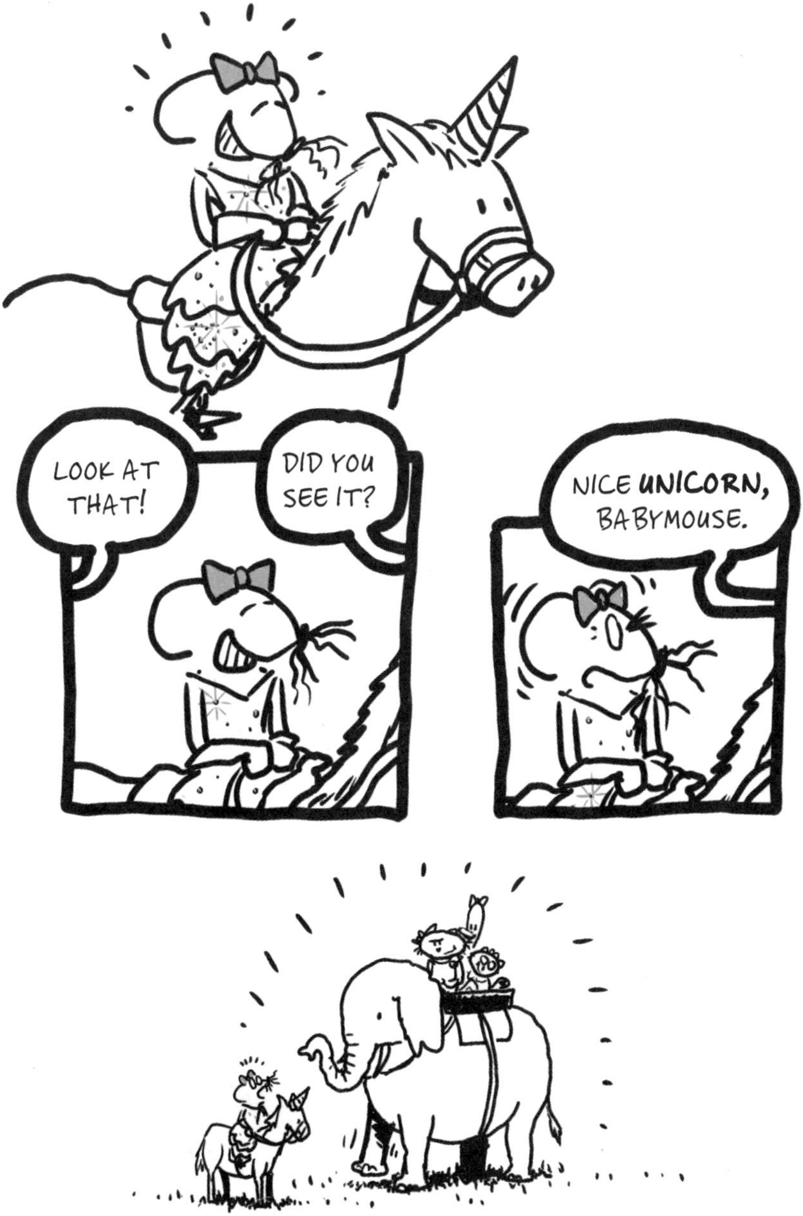
LOOK AT THAT!
DID YOU SEE IT?
NICE **UNICORN,** BABYMOUSE.

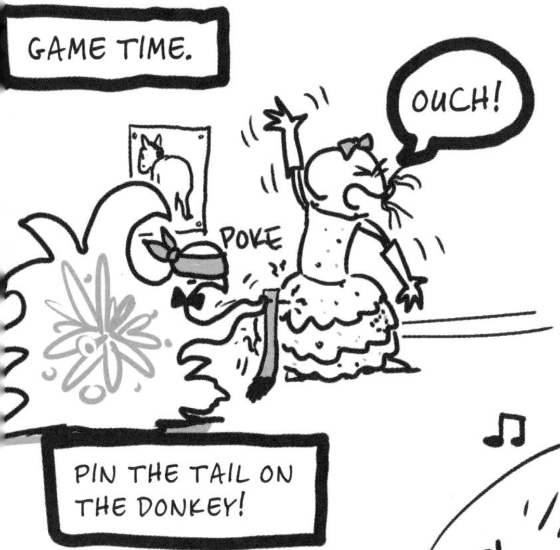
GAME TIME.
OUCH!
POKE
PIN THE TAIL ON THE DONKEY!

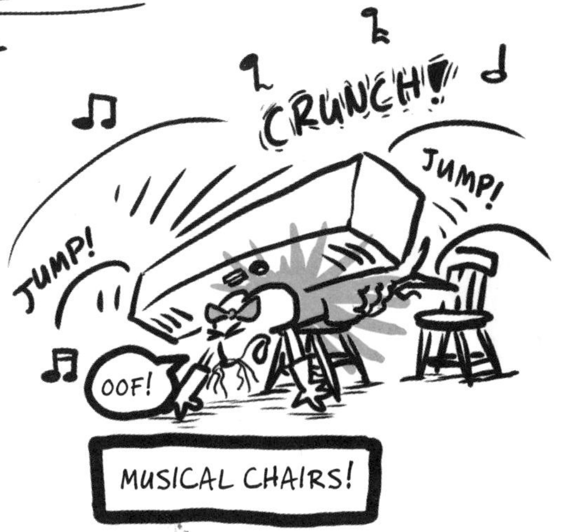
CRUNCH!
JUMP!
JUMP!
OOF!
MUSICAL CHAIRS!

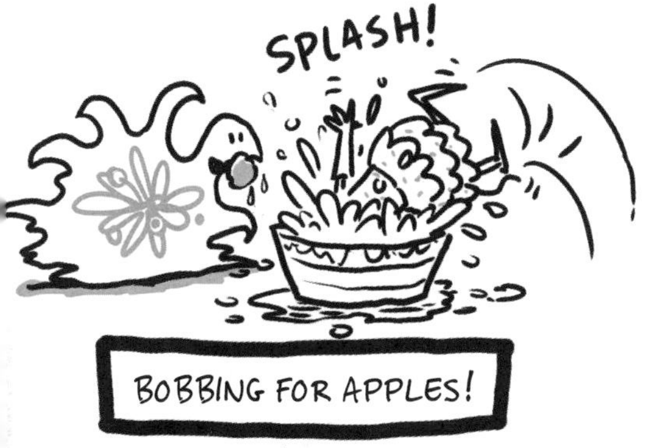
SPLASH!
BOBBING FOR APPLES!

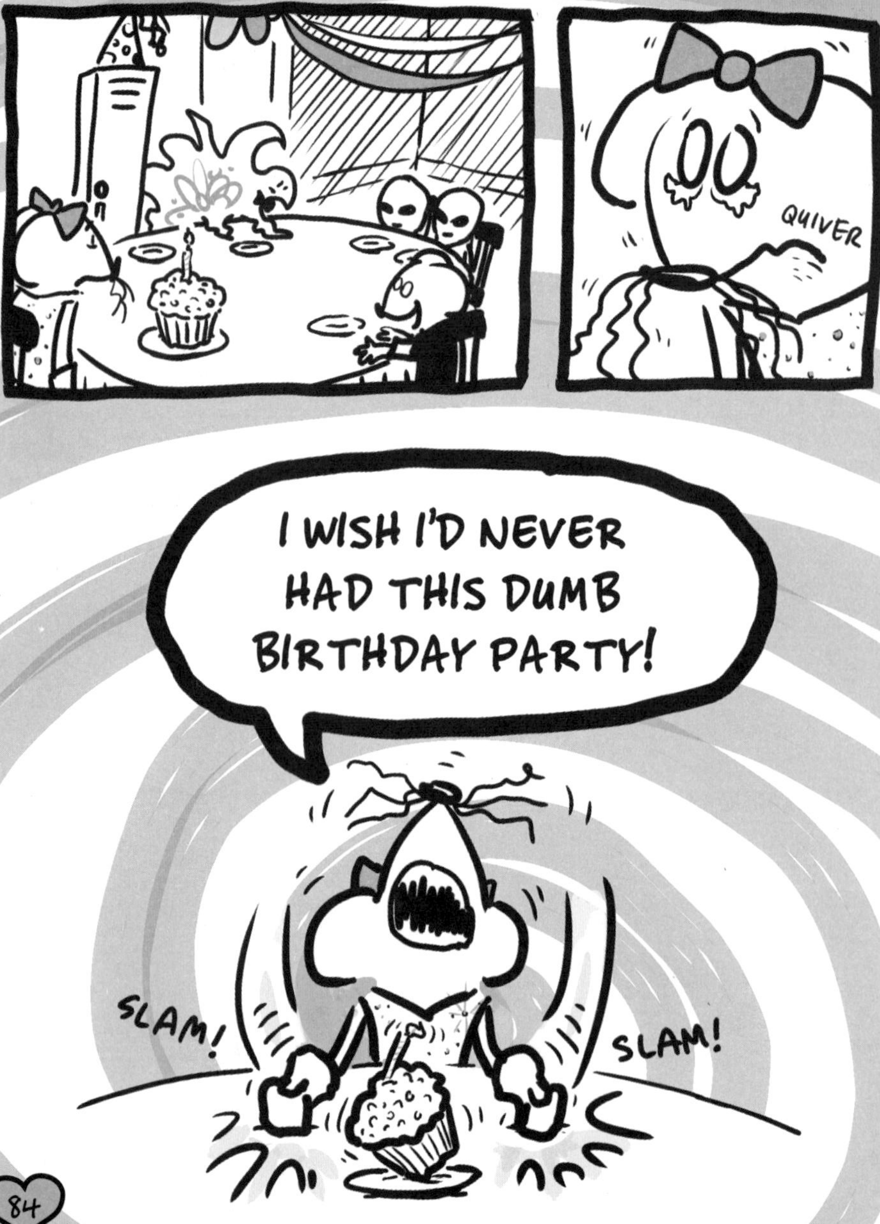
QUIVER
I WISH I'D NEVER HAD THIS DUMB BIRTHDAY PARTY!
SLAM!
SLAM!

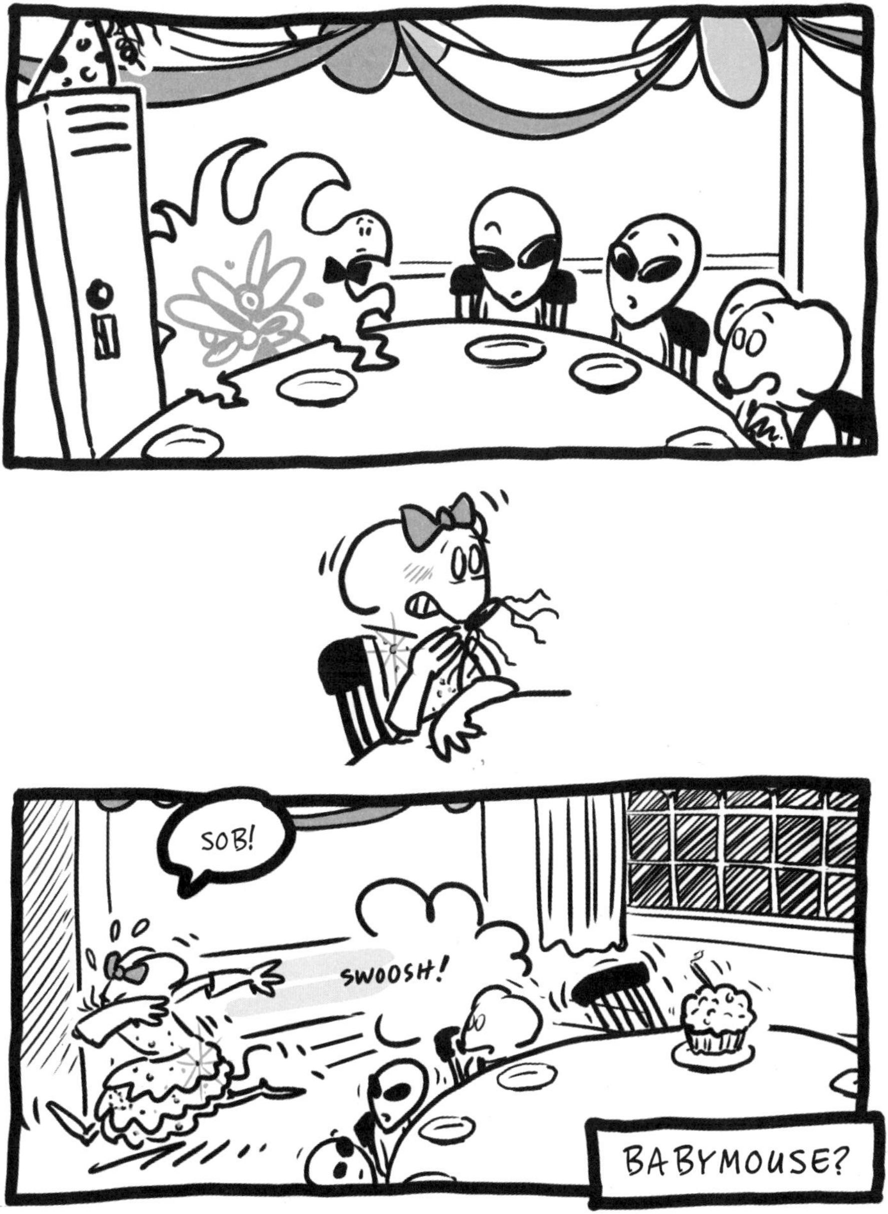
SOB!
SWOOSH!
BABYMOUSE?

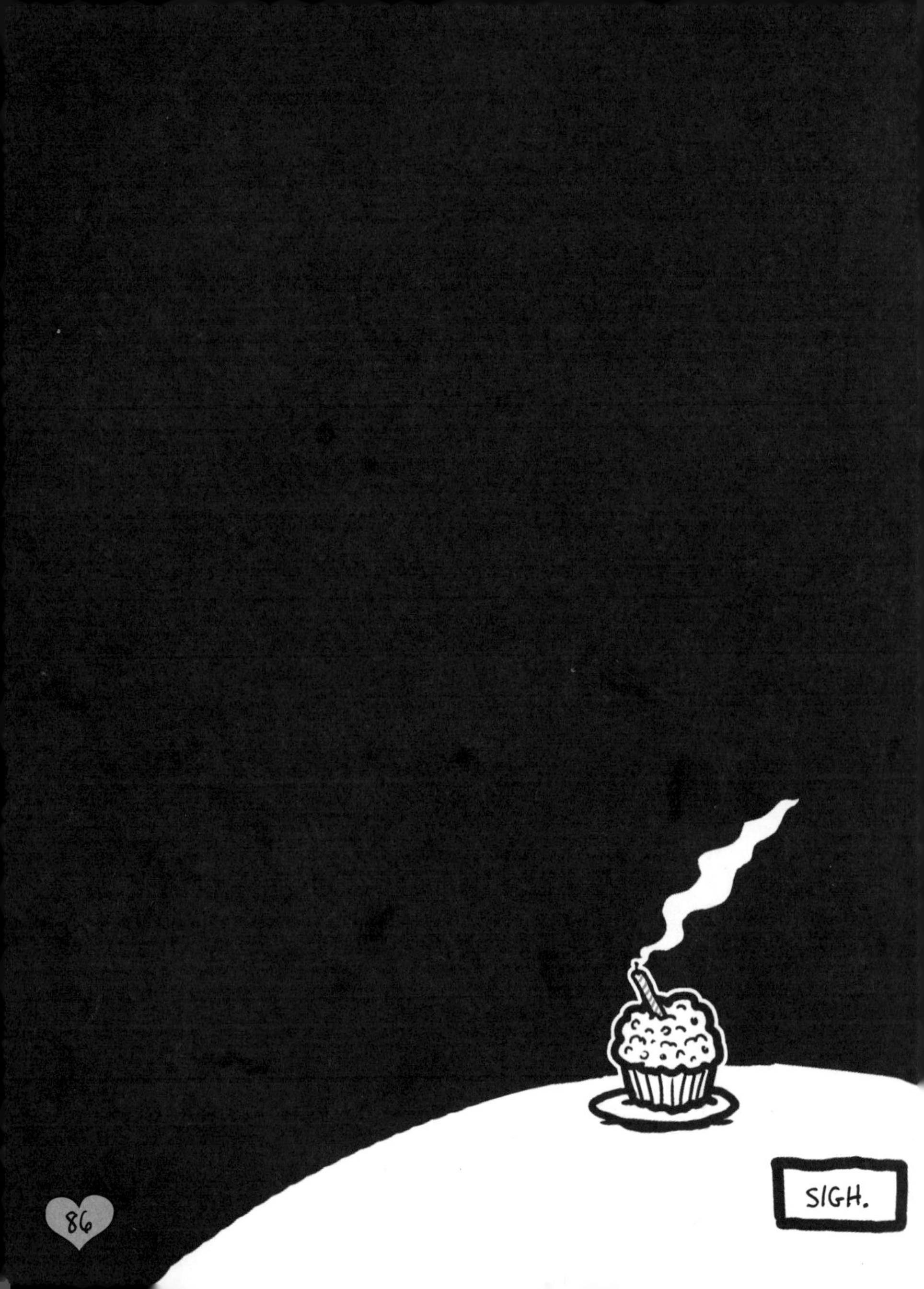
SIGH.

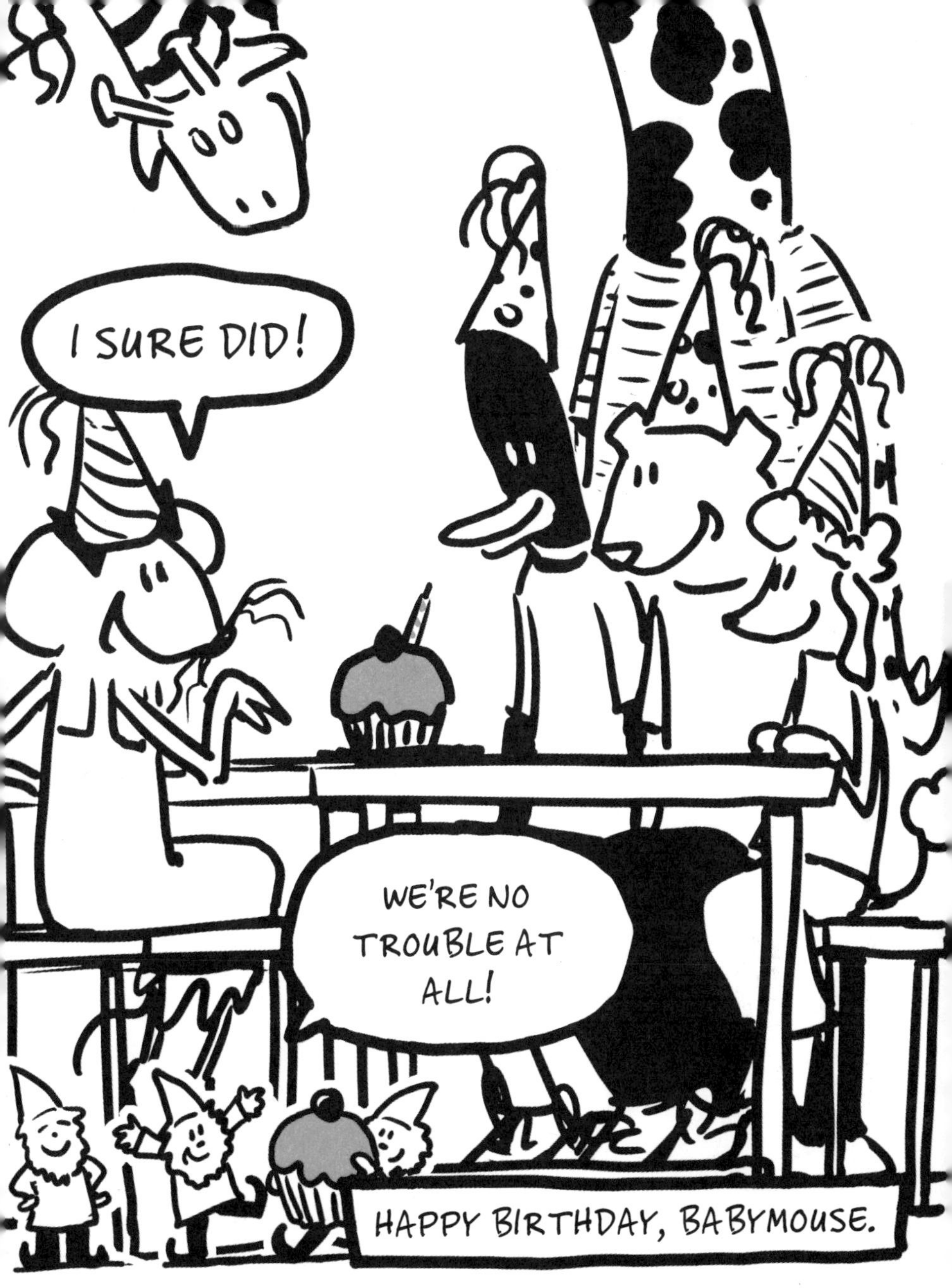
I SURE DID!
WE'RE NO TROUBLE AT ALL!
HAPPY BIRTHDAY, BABYMOUSE.

USA

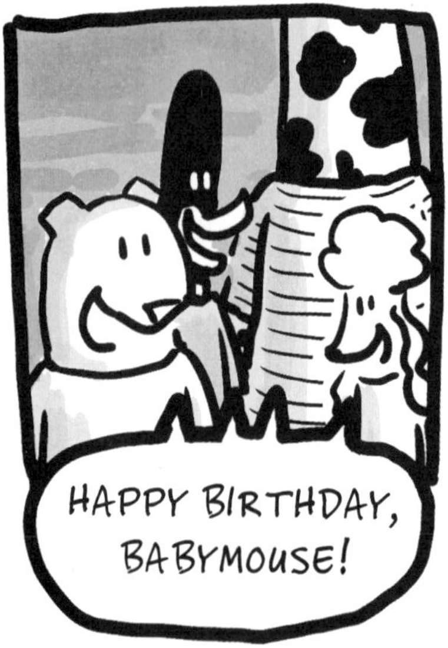
HAPPY BIRTHDAY, BABYMOUSE!

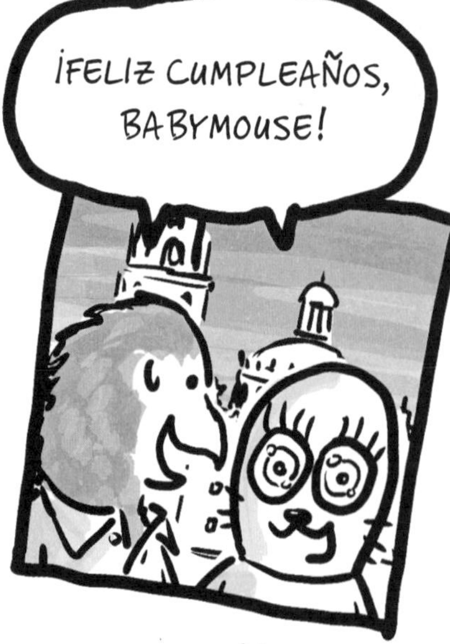
¡FELIZ CUMPLEAÑOS, BABYMOUSE!

MEXICO

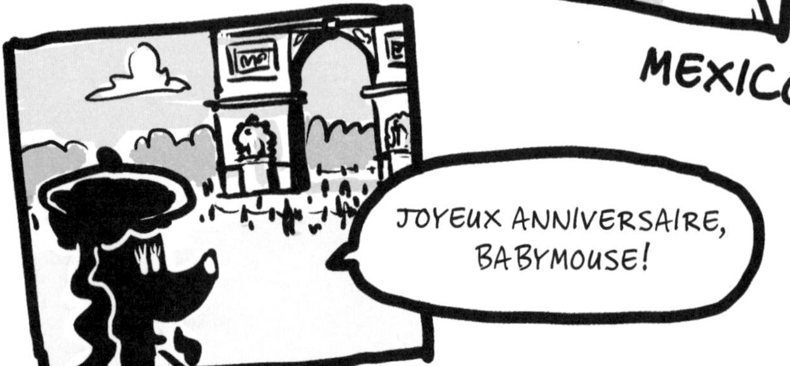
JOYEUX ANNIVERSAIRE, BABYMOUSE!

FRANCE

If you like Babymouse,
you'll love these other great books
by Jennifer L. Holm!

THE BOSTON JANE TRILOGY
EIGHTH GRADE IS MAKING ME SICK
MIDDLE SCHOOL IS WORSE THAN MEATLOAF
OUR ONLY MAY AMELIA
PENNY FROM HEAVEN
TURTLE IN PARADISE

AND DON'T MISS THE **SQUISH** GRAPHIC NOVELS BY MATTHEW HOLM AND JENNIFER L. HOLM:

#1 SQUISH: Super Amoeba

#2 SQUISH: Brave New Pond

#3 SQUISH: The Power of the Parasite

#4 SQUISH: Captain Disaster

#5 SQUISH: Game On!

And coming soon:

#6 SQUISH: Fear the Amoeba